Alphonse Daudet

Tartarin of Tarascon; traveller, 'Turk' and lion-hunter

Alphonse Daudet

Tartarin of Tarascon; traveller, 'Turk' and lion-hunter

ISBN/EAN: 9783337208080

Printed in Europe, USA, Canada, Australia, Japan

Cover: Foto ©Andreas Hilbeck / pixelio.de

More available books at **www.hansebooks.com**

𝔐acmillan's Colonial 𝔏ibrary

Tartarin of Tarascon

Traveller, "Turk"
and Lion-Hunter

By Alphonse Daudet

London
Macmillan and Co. Ltd.
and New York
1896

Printed by BALLANTYNE, HANSON & Co.
At the Ballantyne Press

TO MY FRIEND

GONZAGUE PRIVAT

Contents.

Contents.

EPISODE THE SECOND.

AMONG "THE TURKS."

Contents.

EPISODE THE THIRD.

AMONG THE LIONS

IN TARASCON

I.

The Garden Round the Giant Trees.

My first visit to Tartarin of Tarascon has remained a never-to-be-forgotten date in my life; although quite ten or a dozen years ago, I remember it better than yesterday.

At that time the intrepid Tartarin lived in the third house on the left as the town begins, on the Avignon road. A pretty

little villa in the local style, with a front
garden and a balcony behind, the walls
glaringly white and the venetians very green;
and always about the doorsteps a brood of
little Savoyard shoeblackguards playing hop-
scotch, or dozing in the broad sunshine with
their heads pillowed on their boxes.

Outwardly the dwelling had no remarkable
features, and none would ever believe it the
abode of a hero; but when you stepped
inside, ye gods and little fishes! what a
change! From turret to foundation-stone
—I mean, from cellar to garret,—the whole
building wore a heroic front; even so the
garden!

O that garden of Tartarin's! there's not
its match in Europe! Not a native tree was
there—not one flower of France; nothing
but exotic plants, gum-trees, gourds, cot-
ton - woods, cocoa and cacao, mangoes,
bananas, palms, a baobab, nopals, cacti,
Barbary figs—well, you would believe yourself in the very midst of Central Africa, ten
thousand leagues away. It is but fair to say
that these were none of full growth; indeed,

the cocoa-palms were no bigger than beet-root, and the baobab (*arbos gigantea*—"giant tree," you know) was easily enough circum-scribed by a window-pot; but, notwithstanding this, it was rather a sensation for Tarascon,

and the townsfolk who were admitted on Sundays to the honour of contemplating Tartarin's baobab, went home chokeful of admiration.

Try to conceive my own emotion, which I was bound to feel on that day of days when I crossed through this marvellous garden; and that was capped when I was ushered into the hero's sanctum.

His study, one of the lions—I should say, lions' dens—of the town, was at the end of the garden, its glass door opening right on to the baobab.

You are to picture a capacious apartment adorned with firearms and steel blades from top to bottom: all the weapons of all the countries in the wide world—carbines, rifles, blunderbusses, Corsican, Catalan, and dagger knives, Malay kreeses, revolvers with spring-bayonets, Carib and flint arrows, knuckle-dusters, life-preservers, Hottentot clubs, Mexican lassoes,—now, can you expect me to name the rest? Upon the whole fell a fierce sunlight, which made the blades and the brass butt-plate of the muskets gleam as if all the more to set your flesh creeping. Still, the beholder was soothed a little by the tame air of order and tidiness reigning over the arsenal. Everything was in place, brushed, dusted, labelled, as in a museum; from point to point the eye descried some obliging little card reading :

Poisoned Arrows !
    Do not touch !

Or,

Loaded !
    Take care, please !

If it had not been for these cautions I never should have dared venture in.

In the middle of the room was an occasional table, on which stood a decanter of rum, a siphon of soda-water, a Turkish tobacco-pouch, "Captain Cook's Voyages," the Indian tales of Fenimore Cooper and Gustave Aimard, stories of hunting the bear, eagle, elephant, and so on. Lastly, beside the table sat a man of between forty and forty-five, short, stout, thick-set, ruddy, with flaming eyes and a strong stubbly beard; he wore flannel tights, and was in his shirt

B

sleeves; one hand held a book, and the
other brandished a very large pipe with an
iron bowl-cap. Whilst reading heaven only
knows what startling adventure of scalp-
hunters, he pouted out his lower lip in a
terrifying way, which gave the honest phiz
of the man living placidly on his means the
same impression of kindly ferocity which
abounded throughout the house.

This man was Tartarin himself—the Tartarin of Tarascon, the great, dreadnought,
incomparable Tartarin of Tarascon.

II.

*A general glance bestowed upon the good town
of Tarascon, and a particular one on "the
cap-poppers."*

At the time I am telling of, Tartarin of
Tarascon had not become the present-day
Tartarin, the great one so popular in the
whole South of France; but yet he was even
then the cock of the walk at Tarascon.

Let us show whence arose this sovereignty.

In the first place you must know that
everybody is shooting mad in these parts,

from the greatest to the least. The chase
is the local craze, and so it has ever been
since the mythological times when the
Tarasque, as the county dragon was called,
flourished himself and his tail in the town
marshes, and entertained shooting parties
got up against him. So you see the passion
has lasted a goodish bit.

It follows that, every Sunday morning,
Tarascon flies to arms, lets loose the dogs
of the hunt, and rushes out of its walls, with
game-bag slung and fowling-piece on the
shoulder, together with a hurly-burly of
hounds, cracking of whips, and blowing of
whistles and hunting-horns. It's splendid
to see ! Unfortunately, there's a lack of
game, an absolute dearth.

Stupid as the brute creation is, you can
readily understand that, in time, it learnt
some distrust.

For five leagues around about Tarascon,
forms, lairs, and burrows are empty, and
nesting-places abandoned. You'll not find
a single quail or blackbird, one little leveret,
or the tiniest tit. And yet the pretty hil-

locks are mightily tempting, sweet smelling
as they are of myrtle, lavender, and rose-
mary ; and the fine muscatels plumped out
with sweetness even unto bursting, as they
spread along the banks of the Rhône, are
deucedly tempting too. True, true ; but
Tarascon lies behind all this, and Tarascon
is down in the black books of the world of
fur and feather. The very birds of passage
have ticked it off on their guide-books, and
when the wild ducks, coming down towards
the Camargue in long triangles, spy the
town steeples from afar, the outermost flyers
squawk out loudly :

"Look out ! there's Tarascon ! give Tarascon the go-by, duckies !"

And the flocks take a swerve.

In short, as far as game goes, there's not a
specimen left in the land save one old rogue
of a hare, escaped by miracle from the mas-
sacres, who is stubbornly determined to stick
to it all his life ! He is very well known at
Tarascon, and a name has been given him.
"Rapid" is what they call him. It is known
that he has his form on M. Bompard's

grounds—which, by the way, has doubled, ay, tripled, the value of the property—but nobody has yet managed to lay him low. At present, only two or three inveterate fellows worry themselves about him. The rest have given him up as a bad job, and old Rapid has long ago passed into the legendary world, although your Tarasconer is very slightly superstitious naturally, and would eat cock-robins on toast, or the swallow, which is Our Lady's own bird, for that matter, if he could find any.

"But that won't do!" you will say. Inasmuch as game is so scarce, what can the sportsmen do every Sunday?

What can they do?

Why, goodness gracious! they go out into the real country two or three leagues from town. They gather in knots of five or six, recline tranquilly in the shade of some well, old wall, or olive tree, extract from their game-bags a good-sized piece of boiled beef, raw onions, a sausage, and anchovies, and commence a next to endless snack, washed down with one of those nice Rhône wines,

which sets a toper laughing and singing.
After that, when thoroughly braced up, they
rise. whistle the dogs to heel, set the guns on

half-cock, and go "on the shoot"— another
way of saying that every man plucks off his

cap, "shies" it up with all his might, and
pops it on the fly with No. 5, 6, or 2 shot,
according to what he is loaded for.

The man who lodges most shot in his cap
is hailed as king of the hunt, and stalks back
triumphantly at dusk into Tarascon, with his
riddled cap on the end of his gun-barrel, amid
any quantity of dog-barks and horn-blasts.

It is needless to say that cap-selling is a
fine business in the town.   There are even
some hatters who sell hunting-caps ready
shot, torn, and perforated for the bad shots ;
but the only buyer known is the chemist
Bézuquet.   This *is* dishonourable !

As a marksman at caps, Tartarin of Tarascon never had his match.

Every Sunday morning out he would
march in a new cap, and back he would
strut every Sunday evening with a mere
thing of shreds.   The loft of Baobab Villa
was full of these glorious trophies.   Hence
all Tarascon acknowledged him as master ;
and as Tartarin thoroughly understood hunting, and had read all the handbooks of all
possible kinds of venery, from cap-popping

to Burmese tiger-shooting, the sportsmen
constituted him their great cynegetical judge,
and took him for referee and arbitrator in
all their differences.

Between three and four daily, at Costecalde the gunsmith's, a stout, stern pipe-
smoker might be seen in a green leather-
covered arm-chair in the centre of the shop
crammed with cap - poppers, they all on
foot and wrangling. This was Tartarin of
Tarascon delivering judgment—Nimrod *plus*
Solomon.

III.

*" Naw, naw, naw !"   The general glance
protracted upon the good town.*

AFTER the craze for sporting, the lusty
Tarascon race cherishes one for love ballad-singing.   There's no believing what a
quantity of ballads is used up in that little
region.   All the sentimental stuff turning
into sere and yellow leaves in the oldest
portfolios, are to be found in full pristine
lustre in Tarascon.   Ay, the entire collec-

tion. Every family has its own pet, as is known to the town.

For instance, it is an established fact that this is the chemist Bézuquet's family's :

" Thou art the fair star that I adore ! "

The gunmaker Costecalde's family's:

> "Would'st thou come to the land
> Where the log-cabins rise?"

The official registrar's family's:

> "If I wore a coat of invisible green,
> Do you think for a moment I could be seen?"

And so on for the whole of Tarascon. Two or three times a week there were parties where they were sung. The singularity was their being always the same, and that the honest Tarasconers had never had an inclination to change them during the long, long time they had been harping on them. They were handed down from father to son in the families, without anybody improving on them or Bowdlerising them : they were sacred. Never did it occur to Costecalde's mind to sing the Bézuquets', or the Bézuquets to try Costecalde's. And yet you may believe that they ought to know by heart what they had been singing for two-score years! But, nay! everybody stuck to his own, and they were all contented.

In ballad-singing, as in cap-popping, Tartarin was still the foremost. His superiority

over his fellow-townsmen consisted in his
not having any one song of his own, but
in knowing the lot, the whole, mind you!
But—there's a but—it was the devil's own
work to get him to sing them.

Surfeited early in life with his drawing-
room successes, our hero preferred by far
burying himself in his hunting story-books, or
spending the evening at the club, to making
a personal exhibition before a Nimes piano
between a pair of home - made candles.
These musical parades seemed beneath him.
Nevertheless, at whiles, when there was a
harmonic party at Bézuquet's, he would drop
into the chemist's shop as if by chance, and,
after a deal of pressure, consent to do the
grand duo in *Robert le Diable* with old Madame Bézuquet. Whoso never heard that,
never heard anything! For my part, even
if I lived a hundred years, I should always
see the mighty Tartarin solemnly stepping up
to the piano, setting his arms akimbo, working up his tragic mien, and, beneath the
green reflection from the show-bottles in the
window, trying to give his pleasant visage the

fierce and satanic expression of Robert the
Devil. Hardly would he fall into position
before the whole audience would be shudder-
ing with the foreboding that something un-
common was at hand. After a hush, old
Madame Bézuquet would commence to her
own accompaniment :

"Robert, my love is thine !
    To thee I my faith did plight,
    Thou seest my affright,—
        Mercy for thine own sake,
    And mercy for mine!"

In an undertone she would add : "Now,
then, Tartarin !" Whereupon Tartarin of
Tarascon, with crooked arms, clenched fists,
and quivering nostrils, would roar three times
in a formidable voice, rolling like a thunder-
clap in the bowels of the instrument :

"No! no! no!" which, like the thorough
southerner he was, he pronounced nasally
as "Naw! naw! naw!" Then would old
Madame Bézuquet again sing :

"Mercy for thine own sake,
    And mercy for mine!"

"Naw! naw! naw!" bellowed Tartarin at
his loudest, and there the gem ended.

Not long, you see; but it was so hand-somely voiced forth, so clearly gesticulated, and so diabolical, that a tremor of terror overran the chemist's shop, and the "Naw! naw! naw!" would be encored several times running.

Upon this Tartarin would sponge his brow, smile on the ladies, wink to the sterner sex, and withdraw upon his triumph to go re-mark at the club with a trifling, offhand air:

"I have just come from the Bézuquets', where I was forced to sing 'em the duo from *Robert le Diable*."

The cream of the joke was that he really believed it!

IV.

"They!"

CHIEFLY to the account of these diverse talents did Tartarin owe his lofty position in the town of Tarascon. Talking of captivating, though, this deuce of a fellow knew how to ensnare everybody. Why, the army, at Tarascon, was for Tartarin. The brave commandant, Bravida, honorary captain retired — in the Military Clothing Factory Department—called him a game fellow; and you may well admit that the warrior

C

knew all about game fellows, he played such a capital knife and fork on game of all kinds.

So was the legislature on Tartarin's side. Two or three times, in open court, the old chief judge, Ladevèse, had said, in alluding to him :

" He is a character ! "

Lastly, the masses were for Tartarin. He had become the swell bruiser, the aristocratic pugilist, the crack bully of the local Corinthians for the Tarasconers, from his build, bearing, style—that aspect of a guard's-trumpeter's charger which fears no noise; his reputation as a hero coming from nobody knew whence or for what, and some scramblings for coppers and a few kicks to the little ragamuffins basking at his doorway.

Along the waterside, when Tartarin came home from hunting on Sunday evenings, with his cap on the muzzle of his gun, and his fustian shooting-jacket belted in tightly, the sturdy river-lightermen would respectfully bob, and blinking towards the huge biceps swelling out his arms, would mutter among one another in admiration :

" Now, there's a powerful chap if you like ! he has double-muscles !"

"*Double muscles !*" why, you never heard of such a thing outside of Tarascon !

For all this, with all his numberless parts, double-muscles, the popular favour, and the so precious esteem of brave Commandant Bravida, ex-captain (in the Army Clothing Factory), Tartarin was not happy: this life in a petty town weighed upon him and suffocated him.

The great man of Tarascon was bored in Tarascon.

The fact is, for a heroic temperament like his, a wild adventurous spirit which dreamt of nothing but battles, races across the pampas, mighty battues, desert sands, blizzards and typhoons, it was not enough to go out every Sunday to pop at a cap, and the rest of the time to ladle out casting-votes at the gunmaker's. Poor dear great man ! If this existence were only prolonged, there would be sufficient tedium in it to kill him with consumption.

In vain did he surround himself with

baobabs and other African trees, to widen
his horizon, and some little to forget his club
and the market-place; in vain did he pile
weapon upon wea-
pon, and Malay kreese
upon Malay kreese,
in vain did he cram

with romances, endea-
vouring like the im-
mortal Don Quixote
to wrench himself by
the vigour of his fancy
out of the talons of
pitiless reality. Alas !
all that he did to ap-
pease his thirst for
deeds of daring only
helped to augment it.
The sight of all the
murderous imple-
ments kept him in a perpetual stew of
wrath and exaltation. His revolvers, repeat-
ing rifles, and ducking-guns shouted "Battle!
battle!" out of their mouths. Through the
twigs of his baobab, the tempest of great

voyages and journeys soughed and blew bad
advice. To finish him came Gustave Aimard,
Mayne Reid, and Fenimore Cooper.

Oh, how many times did Tartarin with a
howl spring up on the sultry summer after-
noons, when he was reading alone amidst his
blades, points, and edges; how many times
did he dash down his book and rush to the
wall to unhook a deadly arm! The poor
man forgot he was at home in Tarascon, in
his underclothes, and with a handkerchief
round his head. He would translate his
readings into action, and, goading himself
with his own voice, shout out whilst swinging a battle-axe or tomahawk:

"Now, only let 'em come!"

"Them"? who were they?

Tartarin did not himself any too clearly
understand. "They" was all that should
be attacked and fought with, all that bites,
claws, scalps, whoops, and yells—the Sioux
Indians dancing around the war-stake to
which the unfortunate pale-face prisoner is
lashed. The grizzly of the Rocky Mountains, who wobbles on his hind legs, and

licks himself with a tongue full of blood.
The Touareg, too, in the desert, the Malay
pirate, the brigand of the Abruzzi—in short,
"they" was warfare, travel, adventure, and
glory.

But, alas ! it was to no avail that the fear-
less Tarasconer called for and defied *them ;*
never did they come.   Odsboddikins ! what
would they have come to do in Tarascon ?

Nevertheless, Tartarin always expected to
run up against them, particularly some evening in going to the club.

V.

How Tartarin went round to his club.

LITTLE, indeed, beside Tartarin of Tarascon, arming himself cap-a-pie to go to his
club at nine, an hour after the retreat had
sounded on the bugle, was the Templar
Knight preparing for a sortie upon the
infidel, the Chinese *tiger* equipping himself
for combat, or the Comanche warrior paint-
ing up for going on the war-path.

"All hands make ready for action!" as
the men-of-war's men say.

In his left hand Tartarin took a steel-
pointed knuckle-duster; in the right he carried a sword-cane; in his left pocket a life-
preserver; in the right a revolver. On his
chest, betwixt outer and under garment, lay a
Malay kreese. But never any poisoned arrows
—they are weapons altogether too unfair.

Before starting, in the silence and ob-
scurity of his study, he exercised himself
for a while, warding off imaginary cuts and
thrusts, lunging at the wall, and giving his
muscles play; then he took his master-key
and went through the garden leisurely;
without hurrying, mark you.   "Cool and
calm—British courage, that is the true sort,
gentlemen."   At the garden end he opened
the heavy iron door, violently and abruptly
so that it should slam against the outer wall.
If "they" had been skulking behind it, you
may wager they would have been jam.   Unhappily, they were not there.

The way being open, out Tartarin would
sally, quickly glancing to the right and left, ere
banging the door to and fastening it smartly
with double-locking.   Then, on the way.

Not so much as a cat upon the Avignon

road—all the doors closed, and no lights in
the casements. All was black, except for
the parish lamps, well spaced apart, blinking
in the river mist.

Calm and proud, Tartarin of Tarascon
marched on in the night, ringing his heels
with regularity, and sending sparks out of
the paving-stones with the ferule of his stick.
Whether in avenues, streets, or lanes, he
took care to keep in the middle of the
road—an excellent method of precaution,
allowing one to see danger coming, and,
above all, to avoid any droppings from windows, as happens after dark in Tarascon and
the Old Town of Edinburgh. On seeing so
much prudence in Tartarin, pray do not conclude that Tartarin had any fear—dear, no!
he only was on his guard.

The best proof that Tartarin was not
scared is, that instead of going to the club
by the shortest cut, he went over the town
by the longest and darkest way round,
through a mass of vile, paltry alleys, at the
mouth of which the Rhône could be seen
ominously gleaming. The poor knight con-
stantly hoped that, beyond the turn of one

of these cut-throats' haunts, "they" would leap from the shadow and fall on his back. I warrant you, "they" would have been warmly received, though; but, alack! by reason of some nasty meanness of destiny, never indeed did Tartarin of Tarascon enjoy the luck to meet any ugly customers—not so much as a dog or a drunken man—nothing at all!

Still, there were false alarms somewhiles. He would catch a sound of steps and muffled voices.

"'Ware hawks!" Tartarin would mutter, and stop short, as if taking root on the spot, scrutinising the gloom, sniffing the wind, even glueing his ear to the ground in the orthodox Red Indian mode. The steps would draw nearer, and the voices grow more distinct, till no more doubt was possible. "They" were coming—in fact, here "they" were!

Steady, with eye afire and heaving breast, Tartarin would gather himself like a jaguar in readiness to spring forward whilst uttering his war-cry, when, all of a sudden, out of the thick of the murkiness, he would hear honest

Tarasconian voices quite tranquilly hailing
him with :

"Hullo! you, by Jove! it's Tartarin!
Good night, old fellow!"

Maledictions upon it! it was the chemist
Bézuquet, with his family, coming from singing their family ballad at Costecalde's.

"Oh, good even, good even!" Tartarin
would growl, furious at his blunder, and

plunging fiercely into the gloom with his cane waved on high.

On arriving in the street where stood his club-house, the dauntless one would linger yet a moment, walking up and down before the portals ere entering. But, finally, weary of awaiting "them," and certain "they" would not show "themselves," he would fling a last glare of defiance into the shades and snarl wrathfully :

"Nothing, nothing at all! there never is nothing !"

Upon which double negation, which he meant as a stronger affirmative, the worthy champion would walk in to play his game of beqziue with the commandant.

VI.

The two Tartarins.

Answer me, you will say, how the mischief is it that Tartarin of Tarascon never left Tarascon with all this mania for adventure, need of powerful sensations, and folly about travel, rides, and journeys from the Pole to the Equator?

For that is a fact: up to the age of five-and-forty, the dreadless Tarasconian had never once slept outside his own room. He had not even taken that obligatory trip to Marseilles which every sound Provençal makes upon coming of age. The most of

his knowledge included Beaucaire, and yet
that's not far from Tarascon, there being
merely the bridge to go over. Unfortunately, this rascally bridge has so often
been blown away by the gales, it is so long
and frail, and the Rhône has such a width at
this spot that—well, faith! you understand!
Tartarin of Tarascon preferred *terra firma*.

We are afraid we must make a clean breast
of it: in our hero there were two very distinct characters. Some Father of the Church
has said : " I feel there are two men in me."
He would have spoken truly in saying this
about Tartarin, who carried in his frame the
soul of Don Quixote, the same chivalric im-
pulses, heroic ideal, and crankiness for the
grandiose and romantic; but, worse is the
luck! he had not the body of the celebrated
hidalgo, that thin and meagre apology for a
body, on which material life failed to take
a hold; one that could get through twenty
nights without its breast-plate being un·
buckled off, and forty-eight hours on a
handful of rice. On the contrary, Tartarin's
body was a stout honest bully of a body,

very fat, very weighty, most sensual and fond of coddling, highly touchy, full of low-class appetite and homely requirements—the short, paunchy body on stumps of the immortal Sancho Panza.

Don Quixote and Sancho Panza in the one same man! you will readily comprehend what a cat-and-dog couple they made! what strife! what clapperclawing! Oh, the fine dialogue for Lucian or Saint-Évremond to write, between the two Tartarins—Quixote-Tartarin and Sancho-Tartarin! Quixote-Tartarin firing up on the stories of Gustave Aimard, and shouting: "Up and at 'em!" and Sancho-Tartarin thinking only of the rheumatics ahead, and murmuring: "I mean to stay at home."

THE DUET.

QUIXOTE-TARTARIN.	SANCHO-TARTARIN.
(Highly excited.)	*(Quite calmly.)*
Cover yourself with glory, Tartarin.	Tartarin, cover yourself with flannel.
(Still more excitedly.)	*(Still more calmly)*
O for the terrible double-barrelled rifle! O for bowie-knives, lassoes, and moccasins!	O for the thick knitted waistcoats! and warm knee-caps! O for the welcome padded caps with ear-flaps!

(Above all self-control.)	*(Ringing up the maid.)*
A battle-axe! fetch me a battle-axe!	Now, then, Jeannette, do bring up that chocolate!

Whereupon Jeannette would appear with an unusually good cup of chocolate, just right in warmth, sweetly smelling, and with the play of light on watered silk upon its unctuous surface, and with succulent grilled steak flavoured with anise-seed, which would set Sancho-Tartarin off on the broad grin, and into a laugh that drowned the shouts of Quixote-Tartarin.

Thus it came about that Tartarin of Tarascon never had left Tarascon.

VII.

Tartarin—The Europeans at Shanghai—
Commerce—The Tartars—Can Tartarin
of Tarascon be an Impostor?—The Mirage.

UNDER one conjunction of circumstances,
Tartarin did, however, once almost start out
upon a great voyage.

The three brothers Garcio-Camus, natives
of Tarascon, established in business at
Shanghai, offered him the managership of
one of their branches there. This undoubt-
edly presented the kind of life he hankered

D

after.   Plenty of active business, a whole
army of under-strappers to order about, and
connections with Russia, Persia, Turkey in
Asia—in short, to be a merchant prince.

In Tartarin's mouth, the title of Merchant
Prince thundered out as something stunning!

The house of Garcio-Camus had the further advantage of sometimes being favoured
with a call from the Tartars.   Then the
doors would be slammed shut, all the clerks
flew to arms, up ran the consular flag, and
zizz! phit! bang! out of the windows upon
the Tartars.

I need not tell you with what enthusiasm
Quixote-Tartarin clutched this proposition;
sad to say, Sancho-Tartarin did not see it in
the same light, and, as he was the stronger
party, it never came to anything.   But in the
town there was much talk about it.   Would
he go or would he not?   "I'll lay he will"—
and "I'll wager he won't!"   It was the event
of the week.   In the upshot, Tartarin did
not depart, but the matter redounded to his
credit none the less.   Going or not going
to Shanghai was all one to Tarascon.   Tar-

tarin's journey was so much talked about that people got to believe he had done it and returned, and at the club in the evening members would actually ask for information on life at Shanghai, the manners and customs and climate, about opium, and commerce.

Deeply read up, Tartarin would graciously furnish the particulars desired, and, in the end, the good fellow was not quite sure himself about not having gone to Shanghai, so that, after relating for the hundredth time how the Tartars came down on the trading post, it would most naturally happen him to add :

"Then I made my men take up arms and hoist the consular flag, and zizz! phit! bang! out of the windows upon the Tartars."

On hearing this, the whole club would quiver.

"But according to that, this Tartarin of yours is an awful liar."

"No, no, a thousand times over, no! Tartarin was no liar."

"But the man ought to know that he has never been to Shanghai" ——

"Why, of course, he knows that; but still " ——

"But still," you see—mark that! It is high time for the law to be laid down once for all on the reputation as drawers of the long bow which Northerners fling at Southerners. There are no Baron Munchausens in the south of France, neither at Nîmes nor Marseilles, Toulouse nor Tarascon. The Southerner does not deceive but is self-deceived. He does not always tell the cold-drawn truth, but he believes he does. His falsehood is not any such thing, but a kind of mental mirage.

Yes, purely mirage! The better to follow me, you should actually follow me into the South, and you will see I am right. You have only to look at that Lucifer's own country, where the sun transmogrifies everything, and magnifies it beyond life-size. The little hills of Provence are no bigger than the Butte Montmartre, but they will loom up like the Rocky Mountains; the Square House at Nîmes—a mere model to put on your sideboard—will seem grander than St. Peter's.

You will see—in brief, the only exaggerator in the South is Old Sol, for he does enlarge everything he touches. What was Sparta

in its days of splendour? a pitiful hamlet. What was Athens? at the most, a second-class town; and yet in history both appear

to us as enormous cities. This is a sample
of what the sun can do.

Are you going to be astonished after this
that the same sun falling upon Tarascon
should have made of an ex-captain in the
Army Clothing Factory, like Bravida, the
"brave commandant;" of a sprout an Indian
fig-tree ; and of a man who had missed going
to Shanghai one who had been there ?

VIII.

Mitaine's Menagerie—A Lion from the Atlas at Tarascon — A Solemn and Fearsome Confrontation.

EXHIBITING Tartarin of Tarascon, as we are, in his private life, before Fame kissed his brow and garlanded him with her well-worn laurel wreath, and having narrated his heroic existence in a modest state, his delights and sorrows, his dreams and his hopes, let us hurriedly skip to the grandest pages of his story, and to the singular event which was

to give the first flight to his incomparable
career.

It happened one evening at Costecalde the
gunmaker's, where Tartarin was engaged in
showing several sportsmen the working of the
needle-gun, then in its first novelty. The
door suddenly flew open, and in rushed a
bewildered cap-popper, howling " A lion, a
lion !" General was the alarm, stupor, uproar and tumult. Tartarin prepared to resist
cavalry with the bayonet, whilst Costecalde
ran to shut the door. The sportsman was
surrounded and pressed and questioned, and
here follows what he told them : Mitaine's
Menagerie, returning from Beaucaire Fair,
had consented to stay over a few days at
Tarascon, and was just unpacking, to set up
the show on the Castle-green, with a lot of
boas, seals, crocodiles, and a magnificent
lion from the Atlas Mountains.

An African lion in Tarascon?

Never in the memory of living man had
the like been seen. Hence our dauntless
cap-poppers looked at one another how
proudly ! What a beaming on their sun-

burned visages! and in every nook of Coste-calde's shop what hearty congratulatory grips of the hand were silently exchanged! The sensation was so great and unforeseen that nobody could find a word to say—not even Tartarin.

Blanched and agitated, with the needle-gun still in his fist, he brooded, erect before the counter. A lion from the Atlas Range at pistol range from him, a couple of strides off? a lion, mind you—the beast heroic and ferocious above all others, the King of the Brute Creation, the crowning game of his fancies, something like the leading actor in the ideal company which played such splendid tragedies in his mind's eye. A lion, heaven be thanked! and from the Atlas, to boot! It was more than the great Tartarin could bear.

Suddenly a flush of blood flew into his face. His eyes flashed. With one convulsive movement he shouldered the needle-gun, and turning towards the brave Commandant Bravida (formerly captain — in the Army Clothing Department, please to remember), he thundered to him—

" Let's go have a look at him, commandant."

" Here, here, I say! that's my gun—my needle-gun you are carrying off," timidly ventured the wary Costecalde ; but Tartarin had already got round the corner, with all the cap-poppers proudly lock-stepping behind him.

When they arrived at the menagerie, they found a goodly number of people there. Tarascon, heroic but too long deprived of sensational shows, had rushed upon Mitaine's portable theatre, and had taken it by storm. Hence the voluminous Madame Mitaine was highly contented.   In an Arab costume, her arms bare to the elbow, iron anklets on, a whip in one hand and a plucked though live pullet in the other, the noted lady was doing the honours of the booth to the Tarasconians ; and, as she also had " double muscles," her success was almost as great as her animals'.

The entrance of Tartarin with the gun on his shoulder was a damper.

All our good Tarasconians, who had been quite tranquilly strolling before the cages, unarmed and with no distrust, without even

any idea of danger, felt momentary appre-
hension, naturally enough, on beholding their
mighty Tartarin rush into the enclosure with
his formidable engine of war. There must
be something to fear when a hero like he
was, came weaponed ; so, in a twinkling, all
the space along the cage fronts was cleared.
The youngsters burst out squalling for fear,
and the women looked round for the nearest
way out. The chemist Bézuquet made off
altogether, alleging that he was going home
for his gun.

Gradually, however, Tartarin's bearing restored courage. With head erect, the intrepid
Tarasconian slowly and calmly made the
circuit of the booth, passing the seal's tank
without stopping, glancing disdainfully on the
long box filled with sawdust in which the boa
would digest its raw fowl, and going to take
his stand before the lion's cage.

A terrible and solemn confrontation, this !

The lion of Tarascon and the lion of Africa
face to face !

On the one part, Tartarin erect, with his
hamstrings in tension, and his arms folded

on his gun barrel; on the other, the lion, a
gigantic specimen, humped up in the straw,
with blinking orbs and brutish mien, resting
his huge muzzle and tawny full-bottomed wig
on his forepaws.   Both calm in their gaze.

Singular thing! whether the needle-gun
had given him "the needle," if the popular
idiom is admissible, or that he scented an
enemy of his race, the lion, who had hitherto
regarded the Tarasconians with sovereign
scorn, and yawned in their faces, was all
at once affected by ire.   At first he sniffed;
then he growled hollowly, stretching out his
claws; rising, he tossed his head, shook his
mane, opened a capacious maw, and belched
a deafening roar at Tartarin.

A yell of fright responded, as Tarascon
precipitated itself madly towards the exit,
women and children, lightermen, cap-poppers,
even the brave Commandant Bravida himself.
But, alone, Tartarin of Tarascon had not
budged.   There he stood, firm and resolute,
before the cage, lightnings in his eyes, and
on his lip that gruesome grin with which all
the town was familiar.   In a moment's time,

when all the cap-poppers, some little fortified
by his bearing and the strength of the bars,
re-approached their leader, they heard him
mutter, as he stared Leo out of countenance :

"Now, this is something like a hunt !"

All the rest of that day, never a word
farther could they draw from Tartarin of
Tarascon.

IX.

Singular effects of Mental Mirage.

CONFINING his remarks to the sentence
last recorded, Tartarin had unfortunately
still said overmuch.

On the morrow, there was nothing talked
about through town but the near-at-hand
departure of Tartarin for Algeria and lion-
hunting. You are all witness, dear readers,
that the honest fellow had not breathed a
word on that head; but, you know, the

mirage had its usual effect.   In brief, all
Tarascon spoke of nothing but the departure.

On the Old Walk, at the club, in Costecalde's, friends accosted one another with a
startled aspect :

"And furthermore, you know the news, at
least ? "

"And furthermore, rather ?   Tartarin's setting out, at least ? "

For at Tarascon all phrases begin with
"and furthermore," and conclude with "at
least," with a strong local accent.   Hence,
on this occasion more than upon others,
these peculiarities rang out till the windows
shivered.

The most surprised of men in the town
on hearing that Tartarin was going away to
Africa, was Tartarin himself.   But only see
what vanity is !   Instead of plumply answer-
ing that he was not going at all, and had not
even had the intention, poor Tartarin, on the
first of them mentioning the journey to him,
observed with a neat little evasive air, "Aha !
maybe I shall—but I do not say as much."
The second time, a trifle more familiarised

with the idea, he replied, " Very likely;" and the third time, " It's certain."

Finally, in the evening, at Costecalde's and the club, carried away by the egg-nogg, cheers, and illumination; intoxicated by the impression that bare announcement of his departure had made on the town, the hapless fellow formally declared that he was sick of banging away at caps, and that he would shortly be on the trail of the great lions of the Atlas. A deafening hurrah greeted this assertion. Whereupon more egg-nogg, bravoes, hand-shaking, slappings of the shoulder, and a torchlight serenade up to midnight before Baobab Villa.

It was Sancho-Tartarin who was anything but delighted. This idea of travel in Africa and lion-hunting made him shudder before-hand; and when the house was re-entered, and whilst the complimentary concert was sounding under the windows, he had a dreadful "row" with Quixote-Tartarin, calling him a cracked head, a visionary, imprudent, and thrice an idiot, and detailing by the card all the catastrophes awaiting him on such an

E.

expedition—shipwreck, rheumatism, yellow
fever, dysentery, the black plague, elephan-
tiasis, and the rest of them.

In vain did Quixote-Tartarin vow that he
had not committed any imprudence—that he
would wrap himself up well, and take even
superfluous necessaries with him. Sancho-
Tartarin would listen to nothing. The poor
craven saw himself already torn to tatters by
the lions, or engulfed in the desert sands like
his late royal highness Cambyses, and the
other Tartarin only managed to appease him
a little by explaining that the start was not
immediate, as nothing pressed.

It is clear enough, indeed, that none em-
bark on such an enterprise without some
preparations. A man is bound to know
whither he goes, hang it all ! and not fly off
like a bird. Before anything else, the Tarasconian wanted to peruse the accounts of great
African tourists, the narrations of Mungo
Park, Du Chaillu, Dr. Livingstone, Stanley,
and so on.

In them, he learnt that these daring ex-
plorers, before donning their sandals for

distant excursions, hardened themselves well beforehand to support hunger and thirst, forced marches, and all kinds of privation. Tartarin meant to act like they did, and from that day forward he lived upon water broth alone. The water broth of Tarascon is a few slices of bread drowned in hot water, with a clove of garlic, a pinch of thyme, and a sprig of laurel. Strict diet, at which you may believe poor Sancho made a wry face.

To the regimen of water broth Tartarin of Tarascon joined other wise practices. To break himself into the habit of long marches, he constrained himself to go round the town seven or eight times consecutively every morning, either at the fast walk or run, his elbows well set against his body, and a couple of white pebbles in the mouth, according to the antique usage.

To get inured to fog, dew, and night coolness, he would go down into his garden every dusk, and stop out there till ten or eleven, alone with his gun, on the lookout, behind the baobab.

Finally, so long as Mitaine's wild beast

show tarried in Tarascon, the cap-poppers
who were belated at Costecalde's might spy
in the shadow of the booth, as they crossed
the Castle-green, a mysterious figure stalking
up and down.   It was Tartarin of Tarascon,
habituating himself to hear without emotion
the roarings of the lion in the sombre night.

X.

Before the Start.

PENDING Tartarin's delay of the event by
all sorts of heroic means, all Tarascon kept
an eye upon him, and nothing else was
busied about. Cap-popping was winged,
and ballad-singing dead. The piano in
Bézuquet's shop mouldered away under a
green fungus, and the Spanish flies dried

upon it, belly up. Tartarin's expedition had put a stopper on everything.

Ah, you ought to have seen his success in the parlours. He was snatched away by one from another, fought for, loaned and borrowed, ay, stolen. There was no greater honour for the ladies than to go to Mitaine's Menagerie on Tartarin's arms, and have it explained before the lion's den how such large game are hunted, where they should be aimed at, at how many paces off, if the accidents were numerous, and the like of that.

Tartarin furnished all the elucidation desired. He had read "The Life of Jules Gerard, the Lion-Slayer," and had lion-hunting at his finger ends, as if he had been through it himself. Hence he orated upon these matters with great eloquence.

But where he shone the brightest was at dinner at Chief Judge Ladevèze's, or brave Commandant Bravida's (the former captain in the Army Clothing Factory, you will keep in mind), when coffee came in, and all the chairs were brought up closer together, whilst they chatted of his future hunts.

Thereupon, his elbow on the cloth, his nose over his Mocha, our hero would discourse in a feeling tone of all the dangers awaiting him thereaway. He spoke of the long moonless night lyings-in-wait, the pestilential fens, the rivers envenomed by leaves of poison-plants, the deep snow-drifts, the scorching suns, the scorpions, and rains of grasshoppers; he also descanted on the peculiarities of the great lions of the Atlas, their way of fighting, their phenomenal vigour, and their ferocity in the mating season.

Heating with his own recital, he would rise from table, bounding to the middle of the dining-room, imitating the roar of a lion and the going off of a rifle: crack! bang! the zizz of the explosive bullet—gesticulating and roaring about till he had overset the chairs.

Everybody turned pale around the board: the gentlemen looking at one another and wagging their heads, the ladies shutting their eyes with pretty screams of fright, the elderly men combatively brandishing their canes; and, in the side apartments, the little boys, who had been put to bed betimes, were greatly startled by the sudden outcries and imitated gun-fire, and screamed for lights.

Meanwhile, Tartarin did not start.

XI.

" Let's have it out with swords, gentlemen, not
pins!"

A DELICATE question : whether Tartarin
really had any intention of going, and one
which the historian of Tartarin would be highly
embarrassed to answer. In plain words,
Mitaine's Menagerie had left Tarascon over
three months, and still the lion-slayer had not
started. After all, blinded by a new mirage,
our candid hero may have imagined in per-
fectly good faith that he had gone to Algeria.

On the strength of having related his future
hunts, he may have believed he had performed
them as sincerely as he fancied he had
hoisted the consular flag and fired on the
Tartars, zizz, phit, bang! at Shanghai.

Unfortunately, granting Tartarin was this
time again dupe of an illusion, his fellow-
townsfolk were not. When, after the quarter's
expectation, they perceived that the hunter
had not packed even a collar-box, they commenced murmuring.

"This is going to turn out like the Shanghai expedition," remarked Costecalde, smiling·

The gunsmith's comment was welcomed
all over town, for nobody believed any longer
in their late idol. The simpletons and pol-
troons—all the fellows of Bézuquet's stamp,
whom a flea would put to flight, and who
could not fire a shot without closing their
eyes—were conspicuously pitiless. In the
club-rooms or on the esplanade, they accosted
poor Tartarin with bantering mien:

"And furthermore, when is that trip coming
off?"

In Costecalde's shop, his opinions gained

no credence, for the cap-poppers renounced their chief!

Next, epigrams dropped into the affair. Chief Judge Ladevèse, who willingly paid court in his leisure hours to the native Muse, composed in local dialect a song which won much success. It told of a sportsman called "Master Gervais," whose dreaded rifle was bound to exterminate all the lions in Africa to the very last. Unluckily, this terrible gun was of a strange kind : "though loaded daily, it never *went off.*"

"It never *went off*"—you will catch the drift.

In less than no time, this ditty became popular; and when Tartarin came by, the longshoremen and the little shoeblacks before his door sang in chorus—

> "Muster Jarvey's roifle
> Allus gittin' chaarged ;
> Muster Jarvey's roifle
> 'll hev to git enlaarged ;
> Muster Jarvey's roifle's
> Loaded oft—don't scoff ;
> Muster Jarvey's roifle
> Nivver do go off ! "

But it was shouted out from a safe distance, on account of the double muscles.

Oh, the fragility of Tarascon's fads !

The great object himself feigned to see and hear nothing; but, under the surface, this sullen and venomous petty warfare much afflicted him.   He felt aware that Tarascon was slipping out of his grip, and that popular favour was going to others; and this made him suffer horribly.

Ah, the huge bowl of popularity ! it's all very well to have a seat in front of it, but what a scalding you catch when it is over-turned !

Notwithstanding his pain, Tartarin smiled and peacefully jogged on in the same life as if nothing untoward had happened.   Still, the mask of jovial heedlessness glued by pride on his face would sometimes be suddenly detached.   Then, in lieu of laughter, one saw grief and indignation.   Thus it was that one morning, when the little blackguards yelped " Muster Jarvey's Roifle " beneath his window, the wretches' voices rose even into the poor great man's room, where he was

shaving before the glass. (Tartarin wore a
full beard, but as it grew very thick, he was
obliged to keep it trimmed orderly.)

All at once the window was violently
opened, and Tartarin appeared in shirt-sleeves
and nightcap, smothered in lather, flourishing
his razor and shaving-brush, and roaring with
a formidable voice :

" Let's have it out with swords, gentlemen, not pins ! "

Fine words, worthy of history's record, with only the blemish that they were addressed to little scamps not higher than their boot-boxes, and who were quite incapable of holding a smallsword.

XII.

A memorable Dialogue in the little Baobab Villa.

AMID the general falling off, the army alone stuck out firmly for Tartarin. Brave Commandant Bravida (the former captain in the Army Clothing Department) continued to show him the same esteem as ever. "He's game!" he persisted in saying—an assertion, I beg to believe, fully worth the chemist Bézuquet's. Not once did the brave officer let out any allusion to the trip to Africa; but when the public clamour grew too loud, he determined to have his say.

One evening the luckless Tartarin was in his study, in a brown study himself, when he saw the commandant stride in, stern, wearing black gloves, buttoned up to his ears.

"Tartarin," said the ex-captain authoritatively, "Tartarin, you'll have to go!"

And there he dwelt, erect in the doorway frame, grand and rigid as embodied Duty. Tartarin of Tarascon comprehended all the sense in "Tartarin, you'll have to go!"

Very pale, he rose and looked around with a softened eye upon the cosy snuggery, tightly closed in, full of warmth and tender light— upon the commodious easy chair, his books, the carpet, the white blinds of the windows, beyond which trembled the slender twigs of the little garden. Then, advancing towards the brave officer, he took his hand, grasped it energetically, and said in a voice somewhat tearful, but stoical for all that:

"I *am* going, Bravida."

And go he did, as he said he would. Not

straight off though, for it takes time to get
the paraphernalia together.

To begin with, he ordered of Bompard two
large boxes bound with brass, and an inscrip-
tion to be on them :

TARTARIN, OF TARASCON.

FIREARMS, &c.

The binding in brass and the lettering took
much time.   He also ordered at Tastavin's
a showy album, in which to keep a diary and
his impressions of travel ; for a man cannot
help having an idea or two strike him even
when he is busy lion-hunting.

Next, he had over from Marseilles a downright cargo of tinned eatables, pemmican
compressed in cakes for making soup, a new
pattern shelter-tent, opening out and packing
up in a minute, sea-boots, a couple of umbrellas, a waterproof coat, and blue spectacles
to ward off ophthalmia   To conclude, Bézuquet the chemist made him up a miniature

F

portable medicine chest stuffed with diachylon plaister, arnica, camphor, and medicated vinegar.

Poor Tartarin ! he did not take these safeguards on his own behalf; but he hoped, by dint of precaution and delicate attentions, to allay Sancho-Tartarin's fury, who, since the start was fixed, never left off raging day or night.

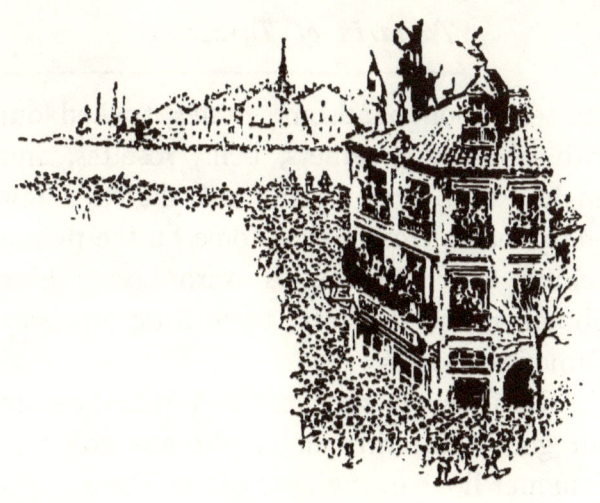

XIII.

The Departure.

EFTSOON arrived the great and solemn
day. From dawn all Tarascon had been on
foot, encumbering the Avignon road and the
approaches to Baobab Villa. People were
up at the windows, on the roofs, and in the
trees; the Rhone bargees, porters, dredgers,
shoe-blacks, gentry, tradesfolk, warpers and
weavers, taffety-workers, the club members,
in short the whole town; moreover, people
from Beaucaire had come over the bridge,
market-gardeners from the environs, carters
in their huge carts with ample tilts, vine-

dressers upon handsome mules, tricked out with ribbons, streamers, bells, rosettes, and jingles, and even, here and there, a few pretty maids from Arles, come on the pillion behind their sweethearts, with bonny blue ribbons round the head, upon little iron-grey Camargue horses.

All this swarm squeezed and jostled before our good Tartarin's door, who was going to slaughter lions in the land of the Turks.

For Tarascon, Algeria, Africa, Greece, Persia, Turkey, and Mesopotamia, all form one great hazy country, almost a myth, called the land of the Turks. They say "*Tur's,*" but that's a linguistic digression.

In the midst of all this throng, the cap-poppers bustled to and fro, proud of their captain's triumph, leaving glorious wakes where they had passed.

In front of the Indian fig-tree house were two large trucks. From time to time the door would open, and allow several persons to be spied, gravely lounging about the little garden. At every new box the throng started and trembled. The articles were named in a loud voice:

"That there's the shelter-tent; these the potted meats; that's the physic-chest; these the gun-cases,"—the cap-poppers giving explanations.

All of a sudden, about ten o'clock, there was a great stir in the multitude, for the garden gate banged open.

"Here he is! here he is!" they shouted.

It was he indeed. When he appeared upon the threshold, two outcries of stupefaction burst from the assemblage :

"He's a Turk!" "He's got on spectacles!"

In truth, Tartarin of Tarascon had deemed it his duty, on going to Algeria, to don the Algerian costume. Full white linen trousers, small tight vest with metal buttons, a red sash two feet wide around the waist, the neck bare and the forehead shaven, and a vast red fez, or *chechia*, on his head, with something like a long blue tassel thereto. Together with this, two heavy guns, one on each shoulder, a broad hunting-knife in the girdle, a bandolier across the breast, a revolver on the hip, swinging in its patent leather case— that is all. No, I cry your pardon, I was forgetting the spectacles—a pantomimically large pair of azure barnacles, which came in patly to temper what was rather too fierce in the bearing of our hero.

"Long life to Tartarin! hip, hip, hurrah for Tartarin!" roared the populace.

The great man smiled, but did not salute, on account of the firearms hindering him. Moreover, he knew now on what popular favour depends; it may even be that in the depths of his soul he cursed his terrible fellow-townsfolk, who obliged him to go away and leave his pretty little pleasure-house with whitened walls and green venetians. But there was no show of this.

Calm and proud, although a little pallid, he stepped out on the footway, glanced at the hand-carts, and, seeing all was right, lustily took the road to the railway-station, without even once looking back towards Baobab Villa. Behind him marched the brave Commandant Bravida, Ladevèze the Chief Judge, Costecalde the gunsmith next, and then all the sportsmen who pop at caps, preceding the hand-carts and the rag, tag, and bobtail. .

Before the station the station-master awaited them, an old African veteran of 1830, who shook Tartarin's hand many times with fervency.

The Paris-to-Marseilles express was not yet in, so Tartarin and his staff went into the waiting-rooms. To prevent the place being overrun, the station-master ordered the gates to be closed.

During a quarter of an hour, Tartarin promenaded up and down in the rooms in the midst of his brother marksmen, speaking to them of his journey and his hunting, and promising to send them skins ; they put their names down in his memorandum-book for a lionskin apiece, as waltzers book for a dance.

Gentle and placid as Socrates on the point of quaffing the hemlock, the intrepid Tarasconian had a word and a smile for each. He spoke simply, with an affable mien ; it looked as if, before departing, he meant to leave behind him a wake of charms, regrets, and pleasant memories. On hearing their leader speak in this way, all the sportsmen felt tears well up, and some were stung with remorse, to wit, Chief Judge Ladevèze and the chemist Bézuquet. The railway employés blubbered in the corners, whilst the outer public squinted through the bars and bellowed : "Long live Tartarin !"

At length the bell rang. A dull rumble was heard, and a piercing whistle shook the vault.

"The Marseilles express, gen'lemen !"

"Good-bye, Tartarin ! Good luck, old fellow ! "

"Good-bye to you all !" murmured the great man, as, with his arms around the brave Commandant Bravida, he embraced his dear native place collectively in him. Then he leaped out upon the platform, and clambered into a carriage full of Parisian ladies, who were ready to die with fright at sight of this stranger with so many pistols and rifles.

XIV.

The Port of Marseilles—" All aboard, all aboard !"

UPON the 1st of December 18—, in clear, brilliant, splendid weather, under a south winter sun, the startled inhabitants of Marseilles beheld a *Turk* come down the Canebière, or their Regent Street. A *Turk*, a regular Turk—never had such a one been seen; and yet, Heaven knows, there is no lack of Turks at Marseilles.

The Turk in question—have I any necessity of telling you it was the great Tartarin of Tarascon?—waddled along the quays, followed by his gun-cases, medicine-chest, and tinned comestibles, to reach the landing-stage of the Touache Company and the mail steamer the *Zouave*, which was to transport him over the sea.

With his ears still ringing with the home applause, intoxicated by the glare of the heavens and the reek of the sea, Tartarin fairly beamed as he stepped out with a lofty head, and between his guns on his shoulders, looking with all his eyes upon that wondrous, dazzling harbour of Marseilles, which he saw for the first time. The poor fellow believed he was dreaming. He fancied his name was Sinbad the Sailor, and that he was roaming in one of those fantastic cities abundant in the "Arabian Nights." As far as eye could reach there spread a forest of masts and spars, cris-crossing in every way.

Flags of all countries floated—English, American, Russian, Swedish, Greek and Tunisian.

The vessels lay alongside the wharves—ay, head on, so that their bowsprits stuck up out over the strand like rows of bayonets. Over it, too, sprawled the mermaids, goddesses, madonnas, and other figure-heads in carved and painted wood which gave names to the ships—all worn by sea-water, split, mildewed, and dripping. Ever and anon, between the hulls, a patch of harbour like watered silk splashed with oil. In the intervals of the yards and booms, what seemed swarms of flies prettily spotted the blue sky. These were the shipboys, hailing one another in all languages.

On the waterside, amidst thick green or black rivulets coming down from the soap-factories loaded with oil and soda, bustled a mass of custom-house officers, messengers, porters, and truckmen with their *bogheys*, or trolleys, drawn by Corsican ponies.

There were shops selling quaint articles, smoky shanties where sailors were cooking their own queer messes, dealers in pipes, monkeys, parrots, ropes, sailcloth, fanciful curios, amongst which were mingled higgledy-piggledy old culverins, huge gilded lanterns, worn-out pulley-blocks, rusty flukeless anchors, chafed cordage, battered speaking-trumpets, and marine glasses almost contemporary with the Ark. Sellers of mussels and clams squatted beside their heaps of shellfish and yawped their goods. Seamen rolled by with tar-pots, smoking soup-bowls, and big baskets full of cuttlefish, from which they went to wash the ink in the milky waters of the fountains.

Everywhere a prodigious collection of all kinds of goods : silks, minerals, wood in stacks, lead in pigs, cloths, sugars, caruba wood logs, colza seed, liquorice sticks, sugar-canes. The East and the West cheek by jowl, even to pyramids of Dutch cheeses which the Genoese were dyeing red by contact with their hands.

Yonder was the corn market : porters discharging sacks down the shoots of lofty elevators upon the pier, and loose grain rolling as a golden torrent through a blonde dust. Men in red skullcaps were sifting it as they caught it in large asses'-skin sieves, and loading it upon carts which took their mill-ward way, followed by a regiment of women and youngsters with wisps and gleaning-baskets. Farther on, the dry docks, where large vessels were laid low on their sides till their yards dipped in the water ; they were

singed with thorn-bushes to free them of sea-
weed; there rose an odour of pitch, and the
deafening clatter of the sheathers coppering
the bottoms with broad sheets of yellow
metal.

At whiles a gap in between the masts, in
which Tartarin could see the haven mouth,
where the vessels came and went: a British
frigate off for Malta, dainty and thoroughly
washed down, with the officer in primrose
gloves, or a large home-port brig hauling out
in the midst of uproar and oaths, whilst the
fat captain, in a high silk hat and frockcoat,
ordered the operations in *Provençal* dialect.
Other craft were making forth under all sail,
and, still farther out, more were slowly
looming up in the sunshine as if they were
sailing in the air.

All the time a frightful riot, the rumbling
of carts, the " Haul all, haul away ! " of the
shipmen, oaths, songs, steamboat whistles,
the bugles and drums in Forts Saint Jean
and Saint Nicolas, the bells of the Major, the
Accoules, and Saint Victor; with the mistral
atop of all, catching up the noises and clamour,

and rolling them up together with a furious
shaking, till confounded with its own voice,
which entoned a mad, wild, heroic melody
like a grand charging tune—one that filled
hearers with a longing to be off, and the
farther the better—a craving for wings.

It was to the sound of this splendid
blast that the intrepid Tartarin of Tarascon
embarked for the land of lions.

EPISODE THE SECOND

AMONG "THE TURKS"

I.

*The Passage—The Five Positions of the Fez—
The Third Evening Out—Mercy upon us!*

JOYFUL would I be, my dear readers, if I
were a painter—a great artist, I mean—in
order to set under your eyes, at the head
of this second episode, the various positions
taken by Tartarin's red cap in the three days'
passage it made on board of the *Zouave*, between France and Algeria.

First would I show you it at the steaming

G

out, upon deck, arrogant and heroic as it
was, forming a glory round that handsome
Tarasconian head.   Next
would I show you it at
the harbour-mouth, when
the bark began to caper
upon the waves ; I would
depict it for you all of
a quake in astonishment,
and as though already ex-
periencing the preliminary
qualms of sea-sickness.

Then, in the Gulf of the Lion, proportion-
ably to the nearing the open sea, where the
white caps heaved harder,
I would make you behold
it wrestling with the tempest, and standing on end
upon the hero's cranium,
with its mighty mane of
blue wool bristling out in
the spray and breeze.

Position Fourth : at six in the afternoon,
with the Corsican coast in view; the unfortunate *chechia* hangs over the ship's side,

and lamentably stares down as though to plumb the depths of ocean. Finally and lastly, the Fifth Position :  at the back of a narrow state-room, in a box-bed so small it seemed one drawer in a nest of them, something shapeless rolled on the pillow with moans of desolation. This was the fez—the fez so defiant at the sailing, now reduced to the vulgar condition of a nightcap, and pulled down over the very ears of the head of a pallid and convulsed sufferer.

How the people of Ta-ascon would have kicked themselves for having con-strained the great Tarta-rin to leave home, if they had but seen him stretched in the bunk in the dull,  wan gleam through the dead-light, amid the sickly odour of cooking and wet wood—the heart-heaving perfume of mail-boats ; if they

had but heard him gurgle at every turn of
the screw, wail for tea every five minutes,
and swear at the steward in a childish treble!

On my word of honour as a story-teller,
the poor *Turk* would have made a paste-
board dummy pity him.

Suddenly, overcome by the nausea, the

hapless victim had not
even the power to un-
do the Algerian girdle-
cloth, or lay aside his
armoury; the lumpy-
handled hunting-
sword pounded his
ribs, and the leather
revolver - case made
his thigh raw.   To finish him arose the
taunts of Sancho-Tartarin, who never ceased
to groan and inveigh :

"Well, for the biggest kind of imbecile,
you are *the* finest specimen!   I told you
truly how it would be.   Ha, ha! you were
bound to go to Africa, of course!   Well,
old merriman, now you are going to Africa,
how do you like it?"

The cruelest part of it was that, from the retreat where he was moaning, the hapless invalid could hear the passengers in the grand saloon laughing, munching, singing, and playing at cards. On board the *Zouave* the company was as jolly as numerous, composed of officers going back to join their regiments, ladies from the Marseilles Alcazar Music Hall, strolling-players, a rich Mussulman returning from Mecca, and a very jocular Montenegrin prince, who favoured them with imitations of the low comedians of Paris. Not one of these jokers felt the sea-sickness, and their time was passed in quaffing champagne with the steamer captain, a good fat born Marseillais, who had a wife and family as well at Algiers as at home, and who answered to the merry name of Barbassou.

Tartarin of Tarascon hated this pack of wretches; their mirthfulness deepened his ails.

At length, on the third afternoon, there was such an extraordinary hullabaloo on the deck that our hero was roused out of his long torpor. The ship's bell was ringing, and the seamen's heavy boots ran over the planks.

"Go ahead! Stop her! Turn astern!" barked the hoarse voice of Captain Barbassou; and then, "Stop her dead!"

There was an abrupt check of movement, a shock, and no more, save the silent rolling of the boat from side to side like a balloon in the air. This strange stillness alarmed the Tarasconian.

"Heaven ha' mercy upon us!" he yelled in a terrifying voice, as, recovering his strength by magic, he bounded out of his berth, and rushed upon deck with his arsenal.

II.

" To arms ! to arms !"

ONLY the arrival, not a foundering.

The *Zouave* was just gliding into the road-stead—a fine one of black, deep water, but dull and still, almost deserted. On elevated ground ahead rose Algiers, the White City, with its little houses of a dead cream-colour huddling against one another lest they slid into the sea. It was like Meudon slope with a laundress's washing hung out to dry. Over it a vast blue satin sky—and such a blue !

A little restored from his fright, the illustrious Tartarin gazed on the landscape, and listened with respect to the Montenegrin prince, who stood by his side, as he named the different parts of the capital, the Kasbah, the upper town, and the Rue Bab-Azoon. A very finely-brought-up prince was this Montenegrin; moreover, knowing Algeria thoroughly, and fluently speaking Arabic. Hence Tartarin thought of cultivating his acquaintance.

All at once, along the bulwark against which they were leaning, the Tarasconian perceived a row of large black hands clinging to it from over the side. Almost instantly a negro's woolly head shot up before him, and, ere he had time to open his mouth, the deck was overwhelmed on every side by a hundred black or yellow desperadoes, half naked, hideous, and fearsome. Tartarin knew who these pirates were— "they," of course, the celebrated "they" who had too often been hunted after by him in the by-ways of Tarascon. At last they had decided to meet him face to face. At the outset surprise nailed him to the spot.

But when he saw the outlaws fall upon the
luggage, tear off the tarpaulin covering, and

actually commence the pillage of the ship,
then the hero awoke. Whipping out his

hunting-sword, "To arms! to arms!" he roared to the passengers; and away he flew, the foremost of all, upon the buccaneers.

"*Ques aco?* What's the stir? What's the matter with you?" exclaimed Captain Barbassou, coming out of the 'tweendecks.

"About time you did turn up, captain! Quick, quick, arm your men!"

"Eh, what for? dash it all!"

"Why, can't you see?"

"See what?"

"There, before you, the corsairs "——

Captain Barbassou stared, bewildered. At this juncture a tall blackamoor tore by with our hero's medicine-chest upon his back.

"You cut-throat! just wait for me!" yelled the Tarasconer as he ran after, with the knife uplifted.

But Barbassou caught him in the spring, and holding him by the waist-sash, bade him be quiet.

"*Tron de ler!* by the throne on high! they're no pirates. It's long since there were any pirates hereabout Those dark porters are light porters. Ha, ha!"

" P—p—porters ? "

" Rather, only come after the luggage to carry it ashore. So put up your cook's galley knife, give me your ticket, and walk off behind that nigger—an honest dog, who will see you to land, and even into a hotel, if you like."

A little abashed, Tartarin handed over his ticket, and falling in behind the representative of the Dark Continent, clambered down by the hanging-ladder into a big skiff dancing alongside. All his effects were already there —boxes, trunks, gun-cases, tinned food,—so cramming up the boat that there was no need to wait for any other passengers. The African scrambled upon the boxes, and squatted there like a baboon, with his knees clutched by his hands. Another negro took the oars. Both laughingly eyed Tartarin, and showed their white teeth.

Standing in the stern-sheets, making that terrifying face which had daunted his fellow-countrymen, the great Tarasconian feverishly fumbled with his hunting-knife haft; for, despite what Barbassou had told him, he

was only half at ease as regarded the intention
of these ebony-skinned porters, who so little
resembled their honest mates of Tarascon.

Five minutes afterwards the skiff landed
Tartarin, and he set foot upon the little
Barbary wharf, where, three hundred years
before, a Spanish galley-slave yclept Miguel
Cervantes devised, under the cane of the
Algerian taskmaster, a sublime romance
which was to bear the title of "Don
Quixote."

III.

*An Invocation to Cervantes—The Disembar-
kation—Where are the Turks?—Not a
sign of them—Disenchantment.*

O MIGUEL CERVANTES SAAVEDRA, if what
is asserted be true, to wit, that wherever
great men have dwelt some emanation of
their spirits wanderingly hovers until the end
of ages, then what remained of your essence
on the Barbary coast must have quivered

with glee on beholding Tartarin of Tarascon disembark, that marvellous type of the
French Southerner, in whom was embodied
both heroes of your work, Don Quixote and
Sancho Panza.

The air was sultry on this occasion. On
the wharf, ablaze with sunshine, were half
a dozen revenue officers, some Algerians ex-
pecting news from France, several squatting
Moors who drew at long pipes, and some
Maltese mariners dragging large nets, between the meshes of which thousands of sar-
dines glittered like small silver coins.

But hardly had Tartarin set foot on earth
before the quay sprang into life and changed
its aspect. A horde of savages, still more
hideous than the pirates upon the steamer,
rose between the stones on the strand and
rushed upon the new-comer. Tall Arabs
were there, nude under woollen blankets,
little Moors in tatters, negroes, Tunisians,
Port Mahonese, M'zabites, hotel servants in
white aprons, all yelling and shouting, hook-
ing on his clothes, fighting over his luggage,
one carrying away the provender, another his

medicine-chest, and pelting him in one fantastic medley with the names of preposterously-entitled hotels.

Bewildered by all this tumult, poor Tartarin wandered to and fro, swore and stormed, went mad, ran after his property, and not

knowing how to make these barbarians understand him, speechified them in French,
Provençal, and even in dog Latin : "*Rosa*, the
rose; *bonus, bona, bonum!*"—all that he knew—
but to no purpose. He was not heeded. Happily, like a god in Homer, intervened a little
fellow in a yellow-collared tunic, and armed
with a long running-footman's cane, who dis-
persed the whole riff-raff with cudgel-play.
He was a policeman of the Algerian capital.
Very politely, he suggested Tartarin should
put up at the Hotel de l'Europe, and he con-
fided him to its waiters, who carted him and
his *impedimenta* thither in several barrows.

At the first steps he took in Algiers, Tartarin of Tarascon opened his eyes widely.
Beforehand he had pictured it as an Oriental
city—a fairy one, mythological, something
between Constantinople and Zanzibar; but
it was back into Tarascon he fell.   Cafés,
restaurants, wide streets, four-storey houses,
a little market-place, macadamised, where the
infantry band played Offenbachian polkas,
whilst fashionably clad gentlemen occupied
chairs, drinking beer and eating pancakes,

some brilliant ladies, some shady ones, and
soldiers—more soldiers—no end of soldiers,
but not a solitary Turk, or, better to say,
there was a solitary Turk, and that was he.

Hence he felt a little abashed about crossing the square, for everybody looked at him.
The musicians stopped, the Offenbachian
polka halting with one foot in the air.

With both guns on his shoulders, and the

H

revolver flapping on his hip, as fierce and
stately as Robinson Crusoe, Tartarin gravely
passed through the groups; but on arriving
at the hotel his powers failed him.   All
spun and mingled in his head : the departure
from Tarascon, the harbour of Marseilles,
the voyage, the Montenegrin prince, the corsairs.   They had to help him up into a room
and disarm and undress him.   They began
to talk of sending for a medical adviser; but
hardly was our hero's head upon the pillow
than he set to snoring, so loudly and so
heartily that the landlord judged the succour
of science useless, and everybody consider-
ately withdrew.

IV.

The First Lying in Wait.

THREE o'clock was striking by the Government clock when Tartarin awoke. He had slept all the evening, night, and morning, and even a goodish piece of the afternoon. It must be granted, though, that in the last three days the red fez had caught it pretty hot and lively !

Our hero's first thought on opening his eyes was, "I am in the land of the lions !" And—well, why should we not say it?—at the idea that lions were nigh hereabouts, within a couple of steps, almost at hand's reach, and that he would have to disentangle a snarled skein with them, ugh! a deadly chill struck him, and he dived intrepidly under the coverlet.

But, before a moment was over, the outward gaiety, the blue sky, the glowing sun that streamed into the bedchamber, a nice little breakfast that he ate in bed, his window wide open upon the sea, the whole flavoured with an uncommonly good bottle of Crescia wine — it very speedily restored him his former pluckiness.

"Let's out and at the lion!" he exclaimed, throwing off the clothes and briskly dressing himself.

His plan was as follows: he would go forth from the city without saying a word to a soul, plunge into the great desert, await nightfall to ambush himself, and bang away at the first lion who walked up. Then would he return to breakfast in the morning at the hotel, receive the felicitations of the natives, and hire a cart to bring in the quarry.

So he hurriedly armed himself, attached

upright on his back the shelter-tent (which, when rolled up, left its centre pole sticking out a clear foot above his head), and descended to the street as stiffly as though he had swallowed it. Not caring to ask the way of anybody, from fear of letting out his project, he turned fairly to the right, and threaded the Bab-Azoon arcade to the very end, where swarms of Algerian Jews watched him pass from their corner ambushes like so many spiders; crossing the Theatre place, he entered the outer ward, and lastly came upon the dusty Mustapha highway.

Upon this was a quaint conglomeration: omnibuses, hackney coaches, *corricolos*, the army service waggons, huge hay-carts drawn by bullocks, squads of Chasseurs d'Afrique, droves of microscopic asses, trucks of Alsatian emigrants, spahis in scarlet cloaks—all filed by in a whirlwind cloud of dust, amidst shouts, songs, and trumpet-calls, between two rows of vile-looking booths, at the doors of which lanky *Mahonnais* women might be seen doing their hair, drinking-dens filled with soldiers, and shops of butchers and knackers.

"What rubbish, to din me about the Orient!" grumbled the great Tartarin; "there are not even as many *Turks* here as at Marseilles."

All of a sudden he saw a splendid camel strut by him quite closely, stretching its long legs and puffing out its throat like a turkey-cock, and that made his heart throb. Camels already, eh? Lions could not be far off now; and, indeed, in five minutes' time he did see a whole band of lion-nunters coming his way under arms.

"Cowards!" thought our hero as he skirted them; "downright cowards, to go at a lion in companies and with dogs!"

For it never could occur to him that any-thing but lions were objects of the chase in Algeria. For all that, these Nimrods wore such complacent phizzes of retired trades-men, and their style of lion-hunting with dogs and game-bags was so patriarchal, that the Tarasconian, a little perplexed, deemed it incumbent to question one of the gentlemen.

"And furthermore, comrade, is the sport good?"

"Not bad," responded the other, regarding the speaker's imposing warlike equipment with a scared eye.

"Killed any?"

"Rather! Not so bad—only look."

Whereupon the Algerian sportsman showed that it was rabbits and woodcock stuffing out the bag.

"What! do you call that your bag? Do you put such-like in your bag?"

"Where else should I put 'em?"

"But it's such little game."

"Some run small and some run large," observed the hunter.

In haste to catch up with his companions, he joined them with several long strides. The dauntless Tartarin remained rooted in the middle of the road with stupefaction.

"Pooh!" he ejaculated, after a moment's reflection, "these are jokers. They haven't killed anything whatever;" and he went his way.

Already the houses became scarcer, and so did the passengers. Dark came on and objects were blurred, though Tartarin walked on for

half an hour more, when he stopped, for it
was night.   A moonless night, too, but
sprinkled with stars.   On the highroad there
was nobody.   The hero concluded that lions
are not stage-coaches, and would not of their
own choice travel the main ways.   So he
wheeled into the fields, where there were
brambles and ditches and bushes at every
step, but he kept on nevertheless.

But suddenly he halted.

"I smell lions about here!" said our
friend, sniffing right and left.

V.

Bang, bang!

CERTAINLY a great wilderness, bristling
with odd plants of that Oriental kind which
look like wicked creatures. Under the feeble
starlight their magnified shadows barred the
ground in every way. On the right loomed
up confusedly the heavy mass of a mountain
—perhaps the Atlas range. On the heart-
hand, the invisible sea hollowly rolling. The
very spot to attract wild beasts.

With one gun laid before him and the
other in his grasp, Tartarin of Tarascon went

down on one knee and waited an hour, ay, a
good couple, and nothing turned up.   Then
he bethought him how, in his books, the
great lion-slayers never went out hunting
without having a lamb or a kid along with
them, which they tied up a space before
them, and set bleating or baa-ing by jerking

its foot with a
string. Not having
any goat, the Ta-
rasconer had the
idea of employing
an imitation, and
he set to crying in
a tremulous voice :
"Baa-a-a !"
At first it was
done very softly,
because at bottom he was a little alarmed lest
the lion should hear him ; but as nothing
came, he baa-ed more loudly.   Still nothing.
Losing patience, he resumed many times running at the top of his voice, till the "Baa, baa,
baa !" came out with so much power that
the goat began to be mistakable for a bull.

Unexpectedly, a few steps in front, some gigantic black thing appeared. He was hushed. This thing lowered its head, sniffed the ground, bounded up, rolled over, and darted off at the gallop, but returned and stopped short. Who could doubt it was the lion? for now its four short legs could plainly be seen, its formidable mane and its large eyes gleaming in the gloom.

Up went his gun into position. Fire's the word! and bang, bang! it was done. And immediately there was a leap back and the drawing of the hunting-knife. To the Tarasconian's shot a terrible roaring replied.

"He's got it!" cried our good Tartarin as, steadying himself on his sturdy supporters, he prepared to receive the brute's charge.

But it had more than its fill, and galloped off, howling. He did not budge, for he expected to see the female mate appear, as the story-books always lay it down she should.

Unhappily, no female came. After two or three hours' waiting the Tarasconian grew tired. The ground was damp, the night was getting cool, and the sea-breeze pricked sharply.

"I have a good mind to take a nap till daylight," he said to himself.

To avoid catching rheumatism, he had recourse to his patent tent. But here's where Old Nick interfered! This tent was of so very ingenious a construction that he could not manage to open it. In vain did he toil over it and perspire an hour through—the confounded apparatus would not come unfolded. There are some umbrellas which amuse themselves under torrential rains with just such tricks upon you. Fairly tired out with the struggle, the victim dashed down the machine and lay upon it, swearing like the regular Southron he was.

" *Tar, tar, rar, tar! tar, rar, tar!* "

"What on earth's that?" wondered Tartarin, suddenly aroused.

It was the bugles of the Chasseurs d'Afrique sounding the turn-out in the Mustapha barracks. The stupefied lion-slayer rubbed his eyes, for he had believed himself out in the boundless wilderness; and do you know where he really was?—in a field of artichokes, between a cabbage-garden and a patch of beets. His Sahara grew kitchen vegetables.

Close to him, on the pretty verdant slope of Upper Mustapha, the snowy villas glowed in the rosy rising sun : anybody would believe himself in the neighbourhood of Marseilles, amongst its *bastides* and *bastidons.*

The commonplace and kitchen-gardenish aspect of this sleep-steeped country much astonished the poor man, and put him in bad humour.

"These folk are crazy," he reasoned, "to plant artichokes in the prowling-ground of lions; for, in short, I have not been dreaming. Lions have come here, and there's the proof."

What he called the proof was blood-spots left behind the beast in its flight. Bending over this ruddy trail, with his eye on the lookout and his revolver in his fist, the valiant Tarasconian went from artichoke to artichoke up to a little field of oats. In the trampled grass was a pool of blood, and in the midst

of the pool, lying on its flank, with a large
wound in the head, was a—guess what?

"A lion, of course!"

Not a bit of it! An ass!—one of those
little donkeys so common in Algeria, where
they are called *bourriquots*.

VI.

*Arrival of the Female—A Terrible Combat—
"Game Fellows Meet Here!"*

LOOKING on his hapless victim, Tartarin's
first impulse was one of vexation. There is
such a wide gap between a lion and poor
Jack! His second feeling was one of pity.
The poor *bourriquot* was so pretty and
looked so kindly. The hide on his still
warm sides heaved and fell like waves. Tartarin knelt down, and strove with the end of

his Algerian sash to stanch the blood; and all you can imagine in the way of touchingness was offered by the picture of this great man tending this little ass.

At the touch of the silky cloth the donkey, who had not twopennyworth of life in him, opened his large grey eye and winked his long ears two or three times, as much as to say, " Oh, thank you !" before a final spasm shook it from head to tail, whereafter it stirred no more.

" Noiraud ! Blackey !" suddenly screamed a voice, choking with anguish, as the branches in a thicket hard by moved at the same time.

Tartarin had no more than enough time to rise and stand upon guard. This was the female !

She rushed up, fearsome and roaring, under form of an old Alsatian woman, her hair in a kerchief, armed with large red umbrella, and calling for her ass, till all the echoes of Mustapha rang. It certainly would have been better for Tartarin to have had to deal with a lioness in fury than this old virago. In vain did the luckless sportsman

try to make her understand how the blunder
had occurred, and he had mistaken "*Noiraud*" for a lion.   The harridan believed he

was making fun of her, and uttering ener-
getical "*Der Teufels!*" fell upon our hero
to bang him with the gingham.   A little

I

bewildered, Tartarin defended himself as best
he could, warding off the blows with his rifle,
streaming with perspiration, panting, jumping
about, and crying out :

"But, Madame, but"——

Much good his buts were ! Madame was
dull of hearing, and her blows continued
hard as ever.

Fortunately a third party arrived on the
battlefield, the Alsatian's husband, of the
same race ; a roadside innkeeper, as well as a
very good ready-reckoner, which was better.
When he saw what kind of a customer he
had to deal with—a slaughterer who only
wanted to pay the value of his victim—he
disarmed his better-half, and they came to
an understanding.

Tartarin gave two hundred francs, the
donkey being worth about ten—at least that
is the current price in the Arab markets.
Then poor Blackey was laid to rest at the
root of a fig-tree, and the Alsatian, raised
to joviality by the colour of the Tarascon
ducats, invited the hero to have a quencher
with him in his wine-shop, which stood only

a few steps off on the edge of the highway. Every Sunday the sportsmen from the city came there to regale of a morning, for the plain abounded with game, and there was no better place for rabbits for two leagues around.

" How about lions ? " inquired Tartarin.

The Alsatian stared at him, greatly as tounded.

" Lions ! "

" Yes, lions. Don't you see them sometimes ? " resumed the poor fellow, with less confidence.

The Boniface burst out in laughter.

" Ho, ho ! bless us ! lions ! What would we do with lions here ? "

" Are there, then, none in Algeria ? "

" 'Pon my faith, I never saw any, albeit I have been twenty years in the colony. Still, I believe I have heard tell of such a thing— leastwise, I fancy the newspapers said—but that is ever so much farther inland—down South, you know " ——

At this point they reached the hostelry a suburban pothouse, with a withered green

bough over the door, crossed billiard-cues
painted on the wall, and this harmless sign
over a picture of wild rabbits feeding:

"GAME FELLOWS MEET HERE."

"Game fellows!"   It made Tartarin think
of Captain Bravida.

VII.

*About an Omnibus, a Moorish Beauty, and a
Wreath of Jessamine.*

COMMON people would have been dis-
couraged by such a first adventure, but men
of Tartarin's mettle do not easily get cast
down.

"The lions are in the South, are they?"
mused the hero. "Very well, then. South
I go."

As soon as he had swallowed his last
mouthful he jumped up, thanked his host,

nodded good-bye to the old hag without any ill-will, dropped a final tear over the hapless Blackey, and quickly returned to Algiers, with the firm intention of packing up and starting that very day for the South.

The Mustapha highroad seemed, unfortunately, to have stretched since overnight; and what a sun and dust there were, and what a weight in that shelter-tent! Tartarin did not feel to have the courage to walk to the town, and he beckoned to the first omnibus coming along, and climbed in.

Oh, our poor Tartarin of Tarascon! how much better it would have been for his name and fame not to have stepped into that fatal ark on wheels, but to have continued on his road afoot, at the risk of falling suffocated beneath the burden of the atmosphere, the tent, and his heavy double-barrelled rifles.

When Tartarin got in the 'bus was full. At the end, with his nose in his prayer-book, sat a large and black-bearded vicar from town; facing him was a young Moorish merchant smoking coarse cigarettes, and a Maltese sailor and four or five Moorish women muffled up in white cloths, so that only their eyes could be spied.

These ladies had been to offer up prayers in
the Abdel Kader cemetery; but this funereal
visit did not seem to have much saddened

them, for they could be heard chuckling and
chattering between themselves under their
coverings whilst munching pastry.   Tartarin

fancied that they watched him narrowly.
One in particular, seated over against him,
had fixed her eyes upon his, and never took
them off all the drive. Although the dame
was veiled, the liveliness of the big black eyes,
lengthened out by *k'hol;* a delightfully slender
wrist loaded with gold bracelets, of which a
glimpse was given from time to time among
the folds; the sound of her voice, the grace-
ful, almost childlike, movements of the head,
all revealed that a young, pretty, and lovable
creature bloomed underneath the veil. The
unfortunate Tartarin did not know where to
shrink. The fond, mute gaze of these splen-
drous Oriental orbs agitated him, perturbed
him, and made him feel like dying with flushes
of heat and fits of cold shivers.

To finish him, the lady's slipper meddled
in the onslaught: he felt the dainty thing
wander and frisk about over his heavy hunting boots like a tiny red mouse. What could
he do? Answer the glance and the pressure,
of course. Ay, but what about the conse-
quences? A loving intrigue in the East is a
terrible matter! With his romantic southern
nature, the honest Tarasconian saw himself

already falling into the grip of the eunuchs, to be decapitated, or better—we mean, worse —than that, sewn up in a leather sack and sunk in the sea with his head under his arm beside him. This somewhat cooled him. In the meantime the little slipper continued its proceedings, and the eyes, widely open opposite him like twin black velvet flowers, seemed to say:

"Come, cull us!"

The 'bus stopped on the Theatre place, at the mouth of the Rue Bab-Azoon. One by one, embedded in their voluminous trousers, and drawing their mufflers around them with wild grace, the Moorish women alighted. Tartarin's confrontatress was the last to rise, and in doing so her countenance skimmed so closely to our hero's that her breath enveloped him—a veritable nosegay of youth and fresh-ness, with an indescribable after-tang of musk, jessamine, and pastry.

The Tarasconian stood out no longer. Intoxicated with love, and ready for anything, he darted out after the beauty. At the rumpling sound of his belts and boots she turned, laid a finger on her veiled mouth, as

who would say, "Hush!" and with the other
hand quickly tossed him a little wreath of
sweet-scented jessamine flowers. Tartarin of
Tarascon stooped to pick it up; but as he
was rather clumsy, and much overburdened
with implements of war, the operation took
rather long. When he did straighten up,
with the jessamine garland upon his heart,
the donatrix had vanished.

VIII.

Ye Lions of the Atlas, repose in peace!

LIONS of the Atlas, sleep !—sleep tranquilly
at the back of your lairs amid the aloes and
cacti. For a few days to come, any way,
Tartarin of Tarascon will not massacre you.
For the time being, all his warlike paraphernalia, gun-cases, medicine-chest, alimentary
preserves, dwelt peacefully under cover in a
corner of room 36 in the Hotel de l'Europe.

Sleep with no fear, great red lions, the

Tarasconian is engaged in looking up that
Moorish charmer. Since the adventure in
the omnibus, the unfortunate swain perpetually fancied he felt the fidgeting of that petty
red mouse upon his huge backwoods trap-
per's foot; and the sea-breeze fanning his
lips was ever scented, do what he would,
with a love-exciting odour of sweetcakes and
patchouli.

He hungered for his indispensable light
of the harem! and he meant to behold her
anew.

But it was no joke of a task. To find
one certain person in a city of a hundred
thousand souls, only known by the eyes,
breath, and slipper,—none but a son of
Tarascon, panoplied by love, would be
capable of attempting such an adventure.

The plague is that, under their broad
white mufflers, all the Moorish women
resemble one another; besides, they do not
go about much, and to see them, a man has
to climb up into the native or upper town
the city of the "Turks," and that is a regular
cut-throat's den.

Little black alleys, very narrow, climbing perpendicularly up between mysterious house-walls, whose roofs lean to touching and form

a tunnel; low doors, and sad, silent little casements well barred and grated. More-over, on both hands, stacks of darksome stalls, wherein ferocious "Turks" smoked long pipes stuck between glittering teeth in piratical heads with white eyes, and mumbled in undertones as if hatching wicked attacks.

To say that Tartarin traversed this grisly place without any emotion would be putting forth falsehood. On the contrary, he was much affected, and the stout fellow only went up the obscure lanes, where his corporation took up all the width, with the utmost precaution, his eye skinned, and his finger on his revolver trigger, in the same manner as he went to the clubhouse at Tarascon. At any moment he expected to have a whole gang of eunuchs and janissaries drop upon his back, yet the longing to behold that dark damsel again gave him a giant's strength and boldness.

For a full week the undaunted Tartarin never quitted the high town. Yes; for all that period he might have been seen cooling his heels before the Turkish bath-houses, awaiting the hour when the ladies came forth in troops, shivering and still redolent of soap and hot water; or squatting at the doorways of mosques, puffing and melting in trying to get out of his big boots in order to enter the temples.

Betimes at nightfall, when he was returning heart-broken at not having discovered anything at either bagnio or mosque, our man from Tarascon, in passing mansions, would hear monotonous songs, smothered twanging of guitars, thumping of tambourines, and feminine laughter-peals, which would make his heart beat.

"Haply she is there!" he would say to himself.

Thereupon, granting the street was unpeopled, he would go up to one of these dwellings, lift the heavy knocker of the low postern, and timidly rap. The songs and merriment would instantly cease. There would be audible behind the wall nothing excepting low, dull flutterings as in a slumbering aviary.

"Let's stick to it, old boy," our hero · would think. "Something will befall us yet."

What most often befell him was the con-
tents of the cold-water jug on the head, or
else peel of oranges and Barbary figs ; never
anything more serious.

Well might the lions of the Atlas Mountains doze in peace.

IX.

Prince Gregory of Montenegro.

It was two long weeks that the unfortunate
Tartarin had been seeking his Algerian flame,
and most likely he would have been seeking
after her to this day if the little god kind to
lovers had not come to his help under the
shape of a Montenegrin nobleman.

It happened as follows.

Every Saturday night in winter there is a
masked ball at the Grand Theatre of Algiers,
just as at the Paris Opera-House. It is the
undying and ever tasteless county fancy dress
ball—very few people on the floor, several

K

castaways from the Parisian students' ball-
rooms or midnight dance-houses, Joans of
Arc following the army, faded characters out
of the Gavarni costume-book of 1840, and
half-a-dozen laundress's underlings who are
aiming to make loftier conquests, but still
preserve a faint perfume of their former life
—garlic and saffron sauce. The real spect-
acle is not there, but in the green-room,
transformed for the nonce into a hall of
green cloth or gaming saloon.

An enfevered and motley mob hustle one
another around the long green table-covers :
Turcos out for the day and staking their double
halfpence, Moorish traders from the native
town, negroes, Maltese, colonists from the
inland, who have come forty leagues in order
to risk on a turning card the price of a plough
or of a yoke of oxen ; all a-quivering, pale,
clenching their teeth, and with that singular,
wavering, sidelong look of the gamester, become a squint from always staring at the
same card in the lay-out.

A little apart are the tribes of Algerian
Jews, playing among acquaintances. The
men are in the Oriental costume, hideously

varied with blue stockings and velvet caps.
The puffy and flabby women sit up stiffly in
tight golden bodices. Grouped around the
tables, the whole tribe wail, squeal, combine,
reckon on the fingers, and play but little. Now
and anon, however, after long conferences,
some old patriarch, with a beard like those of
saints by the Old Masters, detaches himself
from the party and goes to risk the family
duro. As long as the game lasted there
would be a scintillation of Hebraic eyes
directed on the board—dreadful black dia-
monds, which made the gold pieces shiver,
and ended by gently attracting them, as if
drawn by a thread. Then arose wrangles,
quarrels, battles, oaths of every land, mad
outcries in all tongues, knives flashing out,
the guard marching in, and the money
disappearing.

It was into the thick of this saturnalia that
the great Tartarin came straying one evening
to find oblivion and heart's ease.

He was roving alone through the gathering,
brooding about his Moorish beauty, when two
angered voices arose suddenly from a gaming-
table above all the clamour and chink of coin.

"I tell you, M'sieu, that I am twenty francs short!"

"Stuff, M'sieu!"

"Stuff yourself, M'sieu!"

"You shall learn whom you are addressing, M'sieu!"

"I am dying to do that, M'sieu!"

"I am Prince Gregory of Montenegro, M'sieu."

Upon this title Tartarin, much excited, cleft the throng and placed himself in the foremost rank, proud and happy to find his prince again, the Montenegrin noble of such politeness whose acquaintance he had begun on board of the mail steamer. Unfortunately the title of Highness, which had so dazzled the worthy Tarasconian, did not produce the slightest impression upon the Chasseurs officer with whom the noble had his dispute.

"I am much the wiser!" observed the military gentleman sneeringly; and turning to the bystanders he added: "'Prince Gregory of Montenegro'—who knows any such a person? Nobody!"

The indignant Tartarin took one step forward.

"Allow me. I know the *prance*," said he, in a very firm voice, and with his finest Tarasconian accent.

The light cavalry officer eyed him hard for a moment, and then, shrugging his shoulders, returned :

"Come, that is good! Just you two share the twenty francs lacking between you, and let us talk no more on the score."

Whereupon he turned his back upon them and mixed with the crowd. The stormy Tartarin was going to rush after him, but the prince prevented that.

"Let him go. I can manage my own affairs."

Taking the interventionist by the arm, he drew him rapidly out of doors. When they were upon the square, Prince Gregory of Montenegro lifted his hat off, extended his hand to our hero, and as he but dimly remembered his name, he began in a vibrating voice :

"Monsieur Barbarin—— "

"Tartarin !" prompted the other, timidly.

"Tartarin, Barbarin, no matter! Between us henceforward it is a league of life and death ! "

The Montenegrin noble shook his hand
with fierce energy. You may infer that the
Tarasconian was proud.

"*Prance, prance!*" he repeated enthusiastically.

In a quarter of an hour subsequently the
two gentlemen were installed in the Platanes
Restaurant, an agreeable late supper-house,
with terraces running out over the sea, where,
before a hearty Russian salad, seconded by a
nice Crescia wine, they renewed the friendship.

You cannot imagine any one more bewitching than this Montenegrin prince. Slender,
fine, with crisp hair curled by the tongs, shaved
"a week under" and pumice-stoned on that,
bestarred with out-of-the-way decorations, he
had the wily eye, the fondling gestures, and
vaguely the accent of an Italian, which gave
him an air of Cardinal Mazarin without his
chin-tuft and moustaches. He was deeply
versed in the Latin tongues, and lugged in
quotations from Tacitus, Horace, and Cæsar's
Commentaries at every opening.

Of an old noble strain, it appeared that his
brothers had had him exiled at the age of
ten, on account of his liberal opinions, since

which time he had roamed the world for pleasure and instruction as a philosophical noble. A singular coincidence! the prince had spent three years in Tarascon; and as Tartarin

showed amazement at never having met him at the club or on the esplanade, His Highness evasively remarked that he never went about. Through delicacy, the Tarasconian did not dare to question further. All great existences have such mysterious nooks.

To sum up, this Signor Gregory was a very

genial aristocrat.   Whilst sipping the rosy
Crescia juice he patiently listened to Tartarin's expatiating on his lovely Moor, and he
even promised to find her speedily, as he had
full knowledge of the native ladies.

They drank hard and lengthily in toasts to
"The ladies of Algiers" and "The freedom
of Montenegro !"

Outside, upon the terrace, heaved the sea,
and its rollers slapped the strand in the
darkness with much the sound of wet sails
flapping.   The air was warm, and the sky
full of stars.

In the plane-trees a nightingale was piping.

It was Tartarin who paid the piper.

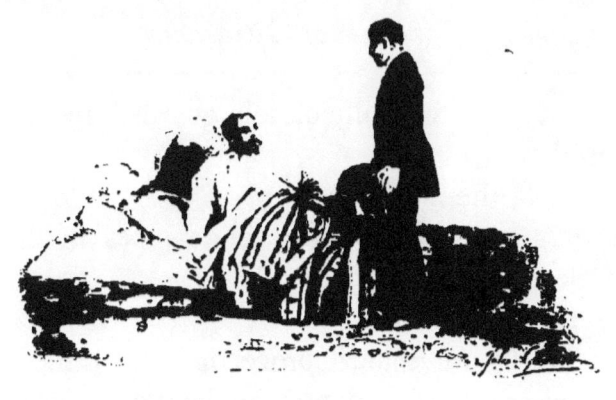

X.

*" Tell me your father's name, and I will tell
you the name of that flower."*

PRINCES of Montenegro are the ones to
find the love-bird.

On the morrow early after this evening
at the Platanes, Prince Gregory was in the
Tarasconian's bedroom.

"Quick! Dress yourself quickly! Your
Moorish beauty is found. Her name is Baya.
She's scarce twenty—as petty as a love, and
already a widow."

"A widow! What a slice of luck!" joyfully
exclaimed Tartarin, who dreaded Oriental
husbands.

"Ay, but woefully closely guarded by her brother."

"Oh, the mischief!"

"A savage chap who vends pipes in the Orléans bazaar."

Here fell a silence.

"A fig for that!" proceeded the prince; "you are not the man to be daunted by such a trifle; and, anyhow, this old corsair can be pacified, I daresay, by having some pipes bought of him. But be quick! On with your courting suit, you lucky dog!"

Pale and agitated, with his heart brimming over with love, the Tarasconian leaped out of his couch, and, as he hastily buttoned up his capacious nether garment, wanted to know how he should act.

"Write straightway to the lady and ask for a tryst."

"Do you mean to say she knows French?" queried the Tarasconian simpleton, with the disappointed mien of one who had believed thoroughly in the Orient.

"Not one word of it," rejoined the prince imperturbably; "but you can dictate the billet-doux, and I will translate it bit by bit."

"O prince, how kind you are!"

The lover began striding up and down the bedroom in silent meditation.

Naturally a man does not write to a Moorish girl in Algiers in the same way as to a seamstress of Beaucaire. It was a very lucky thing that our hero had in mind his numerous readings, which allowed him, by amalgamating the Red Indian eloquence of Gustave Aimard's Apaches with Lamartine's rhetorical flourishes in the "Voyage en Orient," and some reminiscences of the "Song of Songs," to compose the most Eastern letter that you could expect to see. It opened with:

"Like unto the ostrich upon the sandy waste"—

and concluded by:

"Tell me your father's name, and I will tell you the name of that flower."

To this missive the romantic Tartarin would have much liked to join an emblematic bouquet of flowers in the Eastern fashion;

but Prince Gregory thought it better to purchase some pipes at the brother's, which could not fail to soften his wild temper, and would certainly please the lady a very great deal, as she was much of a smoker.

"Let's be off at once to buy them!" said Tartarin, full of ardour.

"No, no! Let me go alone. I can get them cheaper."

"Eh, what? Would you save me the trouble? O prince, prince, you do me proud!"

Quite abashed, the good-hearted fellow offered his purse to the obliging Montenegrin, urging him to overlook nothing by which the lady would be gratified.

Unfortunately the suit, albeit capitally commenced, did not progress as rapidly as might have been anticipated. It appeared that the Moorish beauty was very deeply affected by Tartarin's eloquence, and, for that matter, three-parts won beforehand, so that she wished nothing better than to receive him; but that brother of hers had qualms, and to lull them it was necessary to buy pipes by the dozens; nay, the gross- -

well, we had best say by the shipload at
once.

"What the plague can Baya do with all
these pipes?" poor Tartarin wanted to know

more than once; but he paid the bills all the
same, and without niggardliness.

At length, after having purchased a moun-
tainous stack of pipes and poured forth lakes
of Oriental poesy, an interview was arranged.

I have no need to tell you with what
throbbings of the heart the Tarasconian
prepared himself; with what carefulness he
trimmed, brilliantined, and perfumed his
rough cap-popper's beard, and how he did
not forget—for everything must be thought
of—to slip a spiky life-preserver and two or
three six-shooters into his pockets.

The ever-obliging prince was coming to
this first meeting in the office of interpreter.

The lady dwelt in the upper part of the
town. Before her doorway a boy Moor of
fourteen or less was smoking cigarettes; this
was the brother in question, the celebrated
Ali. On seeing the pair of visitors arrive, he
gave a double knock on the postern gate and
delicately glided away.

The door opened. A negress appeared,
who conducted the gentlemen, without uttering a word, across the narrow inner courtyard into a small cool room, where the lady
awaited them, reclining on a low ottoman.
At first glance she appeared smaller and
stouter than the Moorish damsel met in
the omnibus by the Tarasconian. In fact,
was it really the same? But the doubt

merely flashed through Tartarin's brain like
a stroke of lightning.

The dame was so pretty thus, with her

feet bare, and plump fingers, fine and pink,
loaded with rings. Under her bodice of
gilded cloth and the folds of her flower-

patterned dress was suggested a lovable
creature, rather blessed materially, rounded
everywhere, and nice enough to eat. The
amber mouthpiece of a *narghileh* smoked at
her lips, and enveloped her wholly in a halo
of light-coloured smoke.

On entering, the Tarasconian laid a hand
on his heart and bowed as Moorlike as
possible, whilst rolling his large impassioned
eyes.

Baya gazed on him for a moment without
making any answer; but then, dropping her
pipe-stem, she threw her head back, hid it in
her hands, and they could only see her white
neck rippling with a wild laugh like a bag
full of pearls.

XI.

Sidi Tart'ri Ben Tart'ri.

SHOULD you ever drop into the coffee-houses of the Algerian upper town after dark, even at this day, you would still hear the natives chatting among themselves, with many a wink and slight laugh, of one Sidi Tart'ri Ben Tart'ri, a rich and good-humoured European, who dwelt, a few years back, in that neighbourhood, with a buxom witch of local origin, named Baya.

This Sidi Tart'ri, who has left such a merry

L.

memory around the Kasbah, is no other than
our Tartarin, as will be guessed.

How could you expect things otherwise?
In the lives of heroes, of saints, too, it happens
the same way—there are moments of blind-
ness, perturbation, and weakness. The illustrious Tarasconian was no more exempt from
this than another, and that is the reason
during two months that, oblivious of fame
and lions, he revelled in Oriental amorous-
ness, and dozed, like Hannibal at Capua, in
the delights of Algiers the White.

The good fellow took a pretty little house
in the native style in the heart of the Arab
town, with inner courtyard, banana - trees,
cool verandahs, and fountains. He dwelt,
afar from noise, in company with the Moorish
charmer, a thorough woman to the manner
born, who pulled at her hubble-bubble all
day when she was not eating.

Stretched out on a divan in front of him,
Baya would drone him monotonous tunes
with a guitar in her fist; or else, to distract
her lord and master, favour him with the
Bee Dance, holding a hand-glass up, in which

she reflected her white teeth and the faces she made.

As the Esmeralda did not know a word of French, and Tartarin none in Arabic, the

conversation died away sometimes, and the Tarasconian had plenty of leisure to do penance for the gush of language of which he had been guilty in the shop of Bézuquet the chemist or that of Costecalde the gunmaker.

But this penance was not devoid of charm, for he felt a kind of enjoyable sullenness in dawdling away the whole day without speaking, and in listening to the gurgling of the hookah, the strumming of the guitar, and the faint splashing of the fountain on the mosaic pavement of the yard.

The pipe, the bath, and caresses filled his entire life. They seldom went out of doors. Sometimes, with his lady-love upon a pillion, Sidi Tart'ri would ride upon a sturdy mule to eat pomegranates in a little garden he had purchased in the suburbs. But never, without exception, did he go down into the European quarter. This kind of Algiers appeared to him as ugly and unbearable as a barracks at home, with its Zouaves in revelry, its music-halls crammed with officers, and its everlasting clank of metal sabre-sheaths under the arcades.

The sum total is, that our Tarasconian was very happy.

Sancho-Tartarin particularly, being very

sweet upon Turkish pastry, declared that one
could not be more satisfied than by this
new existence. Quixote-Tartarin had some
twinges at whiles on thinking of Tarascon
and the promises of lion-skins ; but this remorse did not last, and to drive away such
dampening ideas there sufficed one glance
from Baya, or a spoonful of those diabolical
dizzying and odoriferous sweetmeats like
Circe's brews.

In the evening Gregory came to discourse
a little about a free Black Mountain. Of in-
defatigable obligingness, this amiable nobleman filled the functions of an interpreter in
the household, or those of a steward at a
pinch, and all for nothing—for the sheer
pleasure of it. Apart from him, Tartarin
received none but "Turks." All those
fierce-headed pirates who had given him such
frights from the backs of their black stalls
turned out, when once he made their acquaintance, to be good inoffensive tradesmen,
embroiderers, dealers in spice, pipe-mouth-
piece turners — well-bred fellows, humble,
clever, close, and first-class hands at homely

card games. Four or five times a week these
gentry would come and spend the evening
at Sidi Tart'ri's, winning his small change,
eating his cates and dainties, and delicately
retiring on the stroke of ten with thanks to
the Prophet.

Left alone, Sidi Tart'ri and his faithful
spouse by the broomstick wedding would
finish the evening on their terrace, a broad
white roof which overlooked the city.

All around them a thousand of other such
white flats, placid beneath the moonshine,
were descending like steps to the sea. The
breeze carried up tinkling of guitars.

Suddenly, like a shower of firework stars,
a full, clear melody would be softly sprinkled
out from the sky, and on the minaret of the
neighbouring mosque a handsome muezzin
would appear, his blanched form outlined on
the deep blue of the night, as he chanted the
glory of Allah with a marvellous voice, which
filled the horizon.

Thereupon Baya would let go her guitar,
and with her large eyes turned towards the
crier, seem to imbibe the prayer deliciously.

As long as the chant endured she would remain thrilled there in ecstasy, like an Oriental saint. The deeply impressed Tartarin would watch her pray, and conclude that it must be a splendid and powerful creed that could cause such frenzies of faith.

Tarascon, veil thy face! here is a son of thine on the point of becoming a renegade!

XII.

The Latest Intelligence from Tarascon.

PARTING from his little country seat, Sidi
Tart'ri was returning alone on his mule on a
fine afternoon, when the sky was blue and
the zephyrs warm.   His legs were kept wide
apart by ample saddle-bags of esparto cloth,
swelled out with cedrats and water-melons.
Lulled by the ring of his large stirrups, and
rocking his body to the swing and sway-
ing of the beast, the good fellow was thus
traversing an adorable country, with his hands

folded on his paunch, three-quarters gone, through heat, in a comfortable doze. All at once, on entering the town, a deafening appeal aroused him.

"Ahoy! What a monster Fate is! Anybody'd take this for Monsieur Tartarin."

On this name, and at the jolly southern accent, the Tarasconian lifted his head, and perceived, a couple of steps away, the honest tanned visage of Captain Barbassou, master of the *Zouave*, who was taking his absinthe at the door of a little coffee-house.

"Hey! Lord love you, Barbassou!" said Tartarin, pulling up his mule.

Instead of continuing the dialogue, Barbassou stared at him for a space ere he burst into a peal of such hilarity that Sidi Tart'ri sat back dumbfounded on his melons.

"What a stunning turban, my poor Monsieur Tartarin! Is it true, what they say of your having turned Turk? How is little Baya? Is she still singing ' Marco la Bella'?"

"Marco la Bella!" repeated the indignant Tartarin. "I'll have you to know, captain, that the person you mention is an honourable

Moorish lady, and one who does not know a word of French."

"Baya does not know French! What lunatic asylum do you hail from, then?"

The good captain broke into still heartier laughter; but, seeing the chops of poor Sidi Tart'ri fall, he changed his course.

"Howsoever, may happen it is not the same lass. Let's reckon that I have mixed 'em up. Still, mark you, Monsieur Tartarin, you will do well, nonetheless, to distrust Algerian Moors and Montenegrin princes."

Tartarin rose in the stirrups, making a wry face.

"The prince is my friend, captain."

"Come, come, don't wax wrathy. Won't you have some bitters to sweeten you? No? Haven't you anything to say to the folks at home, neither? Well, then, a pleasant journey. By the way, mate, I have some good French 'bacco upon me, and if you would like to carry away a few pipefuls, you have only to take some. Take it, won't you? It's your beastly Oriental 'baccoes that have befogged your brain."

Upon this the captain went back to his absinthe, whilst the moody Tartarin trotted slowly on the road to his little house. Although his great soul refused to credit anything, Barbassou's insinuations had vexed him, and the familiar adjurations and home accent had awakened vague remorse.

He found nobody at home, Baya having gone out to the bath. The negress appeared sinister and the dwelling saddening. A prey to inexpressible melancholy, he went and sat down by the fountain to load a pipe with Barbassou's tobacco. It was wrapped up in a piece of the Marseilles *Sémaphore* newspaper. On flattening it out, the name of his native place struck his eyes.

" *Our Tarascon correspondent writes :*—

"The city is in distress. There has been no news for several months from Tartarin the lion-slayer, who set off to hunt the great feline tribe in Africa. What can have become of our heroic fellow-countryman? Those hardly dare ask who know, as we do, how hot-headed he was, and what boldness and thirst for adventures were his. Has he, like many others, been smothered in the sands, or has he fallen under the murderous fangs of one of those monsters of the Atlas Range of which he had promised the skins to the municipality? What a dreadful state of uncertainty! It is true some negro traders, come to Beaucaire Fair, assert having met in the middle of the deserts a European whose description agreed with his; he was proceeding towards Timbuctoo. May Heaven preserve our Tartarin!"

When he read this, the son of Tarascon reddened, blanched, and shuddered. All Tarascon appeared unto him: the club, the cap-poppers, Costecalde's green arm-chair, and, hovering over all like a spread eagle, the imposing moustaches of brave Commandant Bravida.

At seeing himself here, as he was, cowardly lolling on a mat, whilst his friends believed him slaughtering wild beasts, Tartarin of Tarascon was ashamed of himself, and could have wept had he not been a hero.

Suddenly he leaped up and thundered:

"The lion, the lion! Down with him!"

And dashing into the dusty lumber-hole where mouldered the shelter-tent, the medicine-chest, the potted meats, and the gun-cases, he dragged them out into the middle of the court.

Sancho-Tartarin was no more: Quixote-Tartarin occupied the field of active life.

Only the time to inspect his armament and
stores, don his harness, get into his heavy
boots, scribble a couple of words to confide
Baya to the prince, and slip a few bank-notes
sprinkled with tears into the envelope, and
then the dauntless Tarasconian rolled away
in the stage-coach on the Blidah road, leaving the house to the negress, stupor-stricken
before the pipe, the turban, and babooshes
—all the Moslem shell of Sidi Tart'ri which
sprawled piteously under the little white
trefoils of the gallery.

AMONG THE LIONS

I.

What becomes of the Old Stage-coaches.

COME to look closely at the vehicle, it was an old stage-coach all of the olden time, upholstered in faded deep blue cloth, with those enormous rough woollen balls which, after a few hours' journey, finally establish a raw spot in the small of your back.

Tartarin of Tarascon had a corner of the inside, where he installed himself most free-and-easily; and, preliminarily to inspiring the rank emanations of the great African felines, the hero had to content himself with that homely old odour of the stage-coach, oddly composed of a thousand smells, of man and woman, horses and harness, eatables and mildewed straw.

M

There was a little of everything inside—a
Trappist monk, some Jew merchants, two
fast ladies going to join *their* regiment, the
Third Hussars, a photographic artist from
Orléansville, and so on. But, however charm-
ing and varied was the company, the Tarasconian was not in the mood for chatting; he
remained quite thoughtful, with an arm in
the arm-rest sling-strap and his guns between
his knees.   All churned up his wits—the
precipitate departure, Baya's eyes of jet, the
terrible chase he was about to undertake, to
say nothing of this European coach, with its
Noah's Ark aspect, rediscovered in the heart
of Africa, vaguely recalling the Tarascon of
his youth, with its races in the suburbs, jolly
dinners on the river-side—a throng of memories, in short.

Gradually night came on.   The guard lit
up the lamps.   The rusty *diligence* danced
creakingly on its old springs; the horses
trotted and their bells jangled.   From time
to time in the boot arose a dreadful clank of
iron : that was the war material.

Tartarin of Tarascon, nearly overcome,

dwelt a moment scanning the fellow-pas-
sengers, comically shaken by the jolts, and
dancing before him like the shadows in
galanty-shows, till his eyes grew cloudy and
his mind befogged, and only vaguely he
heard the wheels grind and the sides of the
conveyance squeak complainingly.

Suddenly a voice called Tartarin by his
name, the voice of an old fairy godmother,
hoarse, broken, and cracked.

" Monsieur Tartarin ! " three times.

" Who's calling me ? "

" It's I, Monsieur Tartarin. Don't you
recognise me ? I am the old stage-coach
who used to do the road betwixt Nimes and
Tarascon twenty year agone. How many
times I have carried you and your friends
when you went to shoot at caps over Jonc-
quières or Bellegarde way ! I did not know
you again at the first, on account of your
Turk's cap and the flesh you have accumu-
lated ; but as soon as you began snoring—
what a rascal is good-luck !—I twigged you
straight away."

" All right, that's all right enough ! "

observed the Tarasconian, a shade vexed;
but softening, he added, "But to the point,
my poor old girl; whatever did you come out
here for?"

"Pooh! my good Monsieur Tartarin, I
assure you I never came of my own free
will. As soon as the Beaucaire railway was
finished I was considered good for nought,
and shipped away into Algeria. And I am
not the only one either! Bless you, next to
all the old stage-coaches of France have been
packed off like me. We were regarded as too
much the conservative—'the slow-coaches'—
d'ye see, and now we are here leading the
life of a dog. This is what you in France
call the Algerian railways."

Here the ancient vehicle heaved a long-
drawn sigh before proceeding.

"My wheels and linchpin! Monsieur Tartarin, how I regret my lovely Tarascon! That
was the good time for me, when I was young!
You ought to have seen me starting off in the
morning, washed with no stint of water and
all a-shine, with my wheels freshly varnished,
my lamps blazing like a brace of suns, and

my boot always rubbed up with oil! It was
indeed lovely when the postillion cracked
his whip to the tune of 'Lagadigadeou, the
Tarasque! the Tarasque!' and the guard,
his horn in its sling and laced cap cocked
well over one ear, chucking his little dog,
always in a fury, upon the top, climbed up
himself with a shout : 'Right—away!'

"Then would my four horses dash off to
the medley of bells, barks, and horn-blasts,
and the windows fly open for all Tarascon to
look with pride upon the royal mail coach
dart over the king's highway.

"What a splendid road that was, Monsieur
Tartarin, broad and well kept, with its mile-
stones, its little heaps of road-metal at regular
distances, and its pretty clumps of vines and
olive-trees on either hand ! Then, again, the
roadside inns so close together, and the
changes of horses every five minutes ! And
what jolly, honest chaps my patrons were !—
village mayors and parish priests going up to
Nimes to see their prefect or bishop, taffety-
weavers returning openly from the *Mazet*,
collegians out on holiday leave, peasants in

worked smock-frocks, all fresh shaven for the
occasion that morning; and up above, on the
top, you gentlemen-sportsmen, always in high
spirits, and singing each your own family
ballad to the stars as you came back in the
dark.

" Deary me! it's a change of times now!
Lord knows what rubbish I am carting here,
come from nobody guesses where! They fill
me with small deer, these negroes, Bedouin
Arabs, swashbucklers, adventurers from every
land, and ragged settlers who poison me
with their pipes, and all jabbering a language
that the Tower of Babel itself could make
nothing of! And, furthermore, you should
see how they treat me—I mean, how they
never treat me: never a brush or a wash.
They begrudge me grease for my axles.
Instead of my good fat quiet horses of other
days, little Arab ponies, with the devil in
their frames, who fight and bite, caper as
they run like so many goats, and break my
splatterboard all to smithereens with their
lashing out behind. Ouch! ouch! there
they are at it again!

"And such roads! Just here it is bear-
able, because we are near the governmental
headquarters; but out a bit there's nothing,
Monsieur—not the ghost of a road at all. We
get along as best we can over hill and dale,
over dwarf palms and mastic-trees. Ne'er a
fixed change of horses, the stopping being
at the whim of the guard, now at one farm,
again at another.

"Somewhiles this rogue goes a couple of
leagues out of the way to have a glass of
absinthe or *champoreau* with a chum. After
which, 'Crack on, postillion!' to make up for
the lost time. Though the sun be broiling
and the dust scorching, we whip on! We
catch in the scrub and spill over, but whip
on! We swim rivers, we catch cold, we get
swamped, we drown, but whip! whip! whip!
Then in the evening, streaming—a nice thing
for my age, with my rheumatics—I have to
sleep in the open air of some caravanserai
yard, open to all the winds. In the dead o'
night jackals and hyænas come sniffing of
my body; and the marauders who don't like
dews get into my compartment to keep warm.

"Such is the life I lead, my poor Monsieur Tartarin, and that I shall lead to the day when—burnt up by the sun and rotted by the damp nights until unable to do anything else—I shall fall in some spot of bad road, where the Arabs will boil their *kouskous* with the bones of my old carcass "——

"Blidah! Blidah!" called out the guard as he opened the door.

II.

*A Little Gentleman drops in and "drops
upon" Tartarin.*

VAGUELY through the mud-dimmed glass
Tartarin of Tarascon caught a glimpse of a
second-rate but pretty town market-place,
regular in shape, surrounded by colonnades
and planted with orange-trees, in the midst
of which what seemed toy leaden soldiers
were going through the morning exercise in
the clear roseate mist. The cafés were shed-
ding their shutters. In one corner there was
a vegetable market. It was bewitching, but
it did not smack of lions yet.

"To the South! farther to the South!"

muttered the good old desperado, sinking back in his corner.

At this moment the door opened. A puff of fresh air rushed in, bearing upon its wings, in the perfume of the orange-blossoms, a little person in a brown frock-coat, old and dry, wrinkled and formal, his face no bigger than your fist, his neckcloth of black silk five fingers wide, a notary's letter-case, and umbrella—the very picture of a village solicitor.

On perceiving the Tarasconian's warlike equipment, the little gentleman, who was seated over against him, appeared excessively surprised, and set to studying him with burdensome persistency.

The horses were taken out and the fresh ones put in, whereupon the coach started off again. The little weasel still gazed at Tartarin, who in the end took snuff at it.

"Does this astonish you?" he demanded, staring the little gentleman full in the face in his turn.

"Oh, dear, no! it only annoys me," responded the other, very tranquilly.

And the fact is, that, with his shelter-tent, revolvers, pair of guns in their cases, and hunting-knife, not to speak of his natural corpulence, Tartarin of Tarascon did take up a lot of room.

The little gentleman's reply angered him.

" Do you by any chance fancy that I am going lion-hunting with your umbrella ? " queried the great man haughtily.

The little man looked at his umbrella, smiled blandly, and still with the same lack of emotion, inquired :

"Oho, then you are Monsieur"——

" Tartarin of Tarascon, lion-killer ! "

In uttering these words the dauntless son of Tarascon shook the blue tassel of his fez like a mane.

Through the vehicle was a spell of stupe-faction.

The Trappist brother crossed himself, the dubious women uttered little screams of affright, and the Orléansville photographer bent over towards the lion-slayer, already cherishing the unequalled honour of taking his likeness.

The little gentleman, though, was not awed.

" Do you mean to say that you have killed

many lions, Monsieur Tartarin?" he asked,
very quietly.

The Tarasconian received his charge in
the handsomest manner.

"Is it many have I killed, Monsieur? I
wish you had only as many hairs on your
head as I have killed of them."

All the coach laughed on observing three
yellow bristles standing up on the little gentleman's skull.

In his turn, the Orléansville photographer
struck in :

"Yours must be a terrible profession,
Monsieur Tartarin. You must pass some
ugly moments sometimes. I have heard
that poor Monsieur Bombonnel "——

"Oh, yes, the panther-killer," said Tartarin, rather disdainfully.

"Do you happen to be acquainted with
him?" inquired the insignificant person.

"Eh! of course! Know him? Why, we
have been out on the hunt over twenty times
together."

The little gentleman smiled.

"So you also hunt panthers, Monsieur
Tartarin?" he asked.

"Sometimes, just for pastime," said the fiery Tarasconian. "But," he added, as he tossed his head with a heroic movement that inflamed the heart of the two sweethearts of the regiment, "that's not worth lion-hunting."

"When all's said and done," ventured the photographer, "a panther is nothing but a big cat."

"Right you are!" said Tartarin, not sorry to abate the celebrated Bombonnel's glory a little, particularly in the presence of ladies.

Here the coach stopped. The conductor came to open the door, and addressed the insignificant little gentleman most respectfully, saying :

"We have arrived, Monsieur."

The little gentleman got up, stepped out, and said, before the door was closed again :

"Will you allow me to give you a bit of advice, Monsieur Tartarin?"

"What is it, Monsieur?"

"Faith! you wear the look of a good sort of fellow, so I would, rather than not, let you have it. Get you back quickly to Tarascon, Monsieur Tartarin, for you are wasting your time here. There do remain a few panthers in the colony, but, out upon the big cats! they are too small game for you. As for lion-hunting, that's all over. There are none left in Algeria, my friend Chassaing having lately knocked over the last."

Upon which the little gentleman saluted, closed the door, and trotted away chuckling, with his document-wallet and umbrella.

"Guard," asked Tartarin, screwing up his face contemptuously, "who under the sun is that poor little mannikin?"

"What! don't you know him? Why, that there's Monsieur Bombonnel!"

III.

A Monastery of Lions.

AT Milianah, Tartarin of Tarascon alighted,
leaving the stage-coach to continue its way
towards the South.

Two days' rough jolting, two nights spent
with eyes open to spy out of window if there
were not discoverable the dread figure of a
lion in the fields beyond the road—so much
sleeplessness well deserved some hours' repose. Besides, if we must tell everything,
since his misadventure with Bombonnel, the
outspoken Tartarin felt ill at ease, notwithstanding his weapons, his terrifying visage,
and his red cap, before the Orléansville

photographer and the two ladies fond of
the military.

So he proceeded through the broad streets
of Milianah, full of fine trees and fountains ;
but whilst looking up a suitable hotel, the
poor fellow could not help musing over Bombonnel's words. Suppose they were true !
Suppose there were no more lions in Algeria ?
What would be the good then of so much
running about and fatigue ?

Suddenly, at the turn of a street, our hero
found himself face to face with—with what ?
Guess ! " A donkey, of course ! " A donkey ?
A splendid lion this time, waiting before a
coffee-house door, royally sitting up on his
hind-quarters, with his tawny mane gleaming
in the sun.

" What possessed them to tell me that
there were no more of them ? " exclaimed the
Tarasconian, as he made a backward jump.

On hearing this outcry the lion lowered
his head, and taking up in his mouth a
wooden bowl that was before him on the
footway, humbly held it out towards Tartarin, who was immovable with stupefaction.

A passing Arab tossed a copper into the
bowl, and the lion wagged his tail. Thereupon Tartarin understood it all. He saw
what emotion had prevented him previously
perceiving: that the crowd was gathered

around a poor tame blind lion, and that
two stalwart negroes, armed with staves, were
marching him through the town as a Savoyard
does a marmot.

N

The blood of Tarascon boiled over at once.

"Wretches that you are!" he roared in a voice of thunder, "thus to debase such noble beasts!"

Springing to the lion, he wrenched the loathsome bowl from between his royal jaws. The two Africans, believing they had a thief to contend with, rushed upon the foreigner with uplifted cudgels. There was a dreadful conflict: the blackamoors smiting, the women screaming, and the youngsters laughing. An old Jew cobbler bleated out of the hollow of his stall, "Dake him to the shustish of the beace!" The lion himself, in his dark state, tried to roar as his hapless champion, after a desperate struggle, rolled on the ground among the spilt pence and the sweepings.

At this juncture a man cleft the throng, made the negroes stand back with a word, and the women and urchins with a wave of the hand, lifted up Tartarin, brushed him down, shook him into shape, and sat him breathless upon a corner-post.

"What, *prance*, is it you?" said the good Tartarin, rubbing his ribs.

"Yes, indeed, it is I, my valiant friend. As soon as your letter was received, I entrusted Baya to her brother, hired a post-chaise, flew fifty leagues as fast as a horse could go, and here I am, just in time to snatch you from the brutality of these ruffians. What have you done, in the name of just Heaven, to bring this ugly trouble upon you?"

"What done, prince? It was too much for me to see this unfortunate lion with a begging-bowl in his mouth, humiliated, conquered, buffeted about, set up as a laughing-stock to all this Moslem rabble"——

"But you are wrong, my noble friend On the contrary, this lion is an object of respect and adoration. This is a sacred beast who belongs to a great monastery of lions, founded three hundred years ago by Mahomet Ben Aouda, a kind of fierce and forbidding La Trappe, full of roarings and wild-beastly odours, where strange monks rear and feed lions by hundreds, and send

them out all over Northern Africa, accompanied by begging brothers. The alms they
receive serve for the maintenance of the
monastery and its mosques; and the two
negroes showed so much displeasure just
now because it was their conviction that
the lion under their charge would forthwith
devour them if a single penny of their collection were lost or stolen through any fault
of theirs."

On hearing this incredible and yet vera-
cious story Tartarin of Tarascon was delighted, and sniffed the air noisily.

"What pleases me in this," he remarked,
as the summing up of his opinion, "is that,
whether Monsieur Bombonnel likes it or not,
there are still lions in Algeria "——

"I should think there were!" ejaculated
the prince enthusiastically. "We will start
to-morrow beating up the Shelliff Plain, and
you will see lions enough!"

"What, prince! have you an intention to
go a-hunting, too?"

"Of course! Do you think I am going to
leave you to march by yourself into the heart

of Africa, in the midst of ferocious tribes of whose languages and usages you are ignorant! No, no, illustrious Tartarin, I shall quit you no more. Go where you will, I shall make one of the party."

"O *prance! prance!*"

The beaming Tartarin hugged the devoted Gregory to his breast at the proud thought of his going to have a foreign prince to accompany him in his hunting, after the example of Jules Gerard, Bombonnel, and other famous lion-slayers.

IV.

The Caravan on the March.

LEAVING Milianah at the earliest hour next morning, the intrepid Tartarin and the no less intrepid Prince Gregory descended towards the Shelliff Plain through a delightful gorge shaded with jessamine, carouba, tuyas, and wild olive-trees, between hedges of little native gardens and thousands of merry, lively rills which scampered down from rock to rock with a singing splash—a bit of landscape meet for the Lebanon.

As much loaded with arms as the great Tartarin, Prince Gregory had, over and above that, donned a queer but magnificent military cap, all covered with gold lace and a

trimming of oak-leaves in silver cord, which
gave His Highness the aspect of a Mexican
general or a railway station-master on the
banks of the Danube.

This plague of a cap much puzzled the
beholder; and as he timidly craved some
explanation, the prince gravely answered :

"It is a kind of headgear indispensable
for travel in Algeria."

Whilst brightening up the peak with a
sweep of his sleeve, he instructed his simple
companion in the important part which the
military cap plays in the French connection
with the Arabs, and the terror this article
of army insignia alone has the privilege of
inspiring, so that the Civil Service has been
obliged to put all its employés in caps, from
the extra-copyist to the receiver-general.   To
govern Algeria (the prince is still speaking)
there is no need of a strong head, or even of
any head at all.   A military cap does it alone,
if showy and belaced, and shining at the top
of a non-human *pole*, like Gessler's.

Thus chatting and philosophising, the
caravan proceeded.   The barefooted porters

leaped from rock to rock with ape-like
screams. The gun-cases clanked, and the
guns themselves flashed. The natives who
were passing, salaamed to the ground before
the magic cap. Up above, on the ramparts
of Milianah, the head of the Arab Department, who was out for an airing with his
wife, hearing these unusual noises, and seeing the weapons gleam between the branches,
fancied there was a revolt, and ordered the
drawbridge to be raised, the general alarm to
be sounded, and the whole town put under a
state of siege.

A capital commencement for the caravan !

Unfortunately, before the day ended, things
went wrong. Of the black luggage-bearers,
one was doubled up with atrocious colics
from having eaten the diachylon out of the
medicine-chest ; another fell on the roadside
dead drunk with camphorated brandy ; the
third, carrier of the travelling-album, de-
ceived by the gilding on the clasps into the
persuasion that he was flying with the trea-
sures of Mecca, ran off into the Zaccar on
his best legs.

This required consideration. The caravan halted, and held a council in the broken shadow of an old fig-tree.

"It's my advice that we turn up negro porters from this even-ing forward," said the prince, trying without success to melt a cake of compressed meat in an improved patent triple-bottomed sauce-pan. "There is, haply, an Arab trader quite near here. The best thing to do is to stop there, and buy some donkeys."

"No, no; no donkeys," quickly inter-rupted Tartarin, be-coming quite red at memory of Noiraud. "How can you ex-pect," he added, hypo-crite that he was, "that such little beasts could carry all our apparatus?"

carry all our apparatus?"

The prince smiled.

"You are making a mistake, my illustrious

friend. However weakly and meagre the
Algerian *bourriquot* may appear to you, he
has solid loins. He must have them so
to support all that he does. Just ask the
Arabs. Hark to how they explain the
French colonial organisation. 'On the top,'
they say, 'is Mossoo, the Governor, with a
heavy club to rap the staff; the staff, for
revenge, canes the soldier;
the soldier clubs the set-
tler, and he hammers the
Arab; the Arab smites the
negro, the negro beats the
Jew, and he takes it out
of the donkey. The poor
bourriquot, having nobody
to belabour, arches up
his back and bears it all.'

You see clearly now that he can bear your
boxes."

"All the same," remonstrated Tartarin,
"it strikes me that jackasses will not chime
in nicely with the effect of our caravan. I
want something more Oriental. For instance,
if we could only get a camel "——

"As many as you like," said His Highness; and off they started for the Arab mart.

It was held a few miles away, on the banks of the Shelliff. There were five or six thousand Arabs in tatters here, grovelling in the sunshine and noisily trafficking, amid jars of black olives, pots of honey, bags of spices, and great heaps of cigars; huge fires were roasting whole sheep, basted with butter; in open air slaughter-houses stark naked negroes, with ruddy arms and their feet in gore, were cutting up kids hanging from crosspoles, with small knives.

In one corner, under a tent patched with a thousand colours, a Moorish clerk of the market in spectacles scrawled in a large book. Here was a cluster of men shouting with rage : it was a spinning-jenny game, set on a corn-measure, and Kabyles were ready to cut one another's throats over it. Yonder were laughs and contortions of delight : it was a Jew trader on a mule drowning in the Shelliff. Then there were dogs, scorpions, ravens, and flies—rather flies than anything else.

But a plentiful lack of camels abounded.

They finally unearthed one, though, of which
the M'zabites were trying to get rid—the real

ship of the desert, the classical, standard
camel, bald, woe-begone, with a long Bedouin

head, and its hump, become limp in conse-
quence of unduly long fasts, hanging melan-
cholically on one side.

Tartarin considered it so handsome that
he wanted the entire party to get upon it.
Still his Oriental craze!

The beast knelt down for them to strap on
the boxes.

The prince enthroned himself on the
animal's neck. For the sake of the greater
majesty, Tartarin got them to hoist him on
the top of the hump between two boxes,
where, proud, and cosily settled down, he
saluted the whole market with a lofty wave of
the hand, and gave the signal of departure.

Thunderation! if the people of Tarascon
could only have seen him!

The camel rose, straightened up its long
knotty legs, and stepped out.

Oh, stupor! At the end of a few strides
Tartarin felt he was losing colour, and the
heroic *chechia* assumed one by one its former
positions in the days of sailing in the *Zouave*.
This devil's own camel pitched and tossed
like a frigate.

" *Prance! prance!* " gasped Tartarin, pallid as a ghost, as he clung to the dry tuft of the hump, "*prance*, let's get down. I find—I feel that I m—m—must get off, or I shall disgrace France."

A deal of good that talk was—the camel was on the go, and nothing could stop it. Behind it raced four thousand barefooted Arabs, waving their hands and laughing like mad, so that they made six hundred thousand white teeth glitter in the sun.

The great man of Tarascon had to resign himself to circumstances. He sadly collapsed on the hump, where the fez took all the positions it fancied, and France was disgraced.

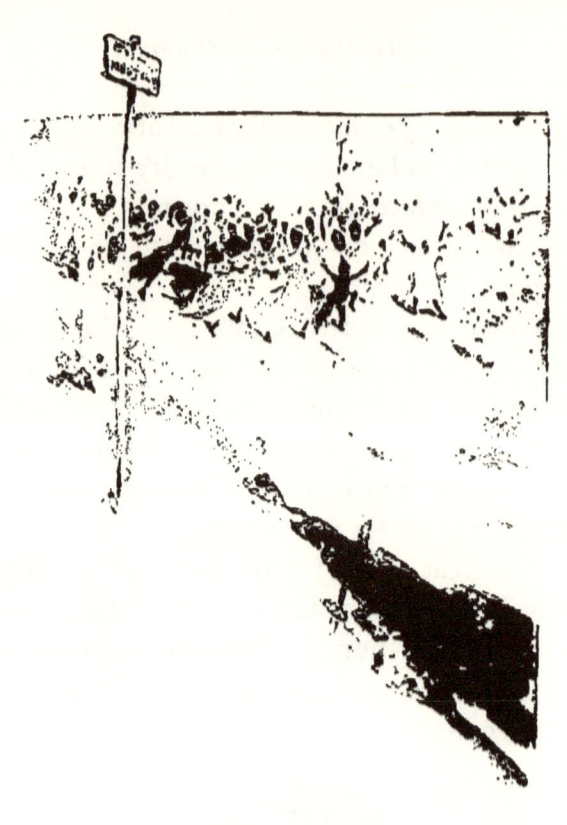

V.

The Night-watch in a Poison-tree Grove.

SWEETLY picturesque as was their new
steed, our lion-hunters had to give it up,
purely out of consideration for the red cap,
of course. So they continued the journey
on foot as before, the caravan tranquilly proceeding southwardly by short stages, the
Tarasconian in the van, the Montenegrin in

the rear, and the camel, with the weapons in their cases, in the ranks.

The expedition lasted nearly a month.

During that seeking for lions which he never found, the dreadful Tartarin roamed from *douar* to *douar* on the immense plain of the Shelliff, through the odd but formidable French Algeria, where the old Oriental perfumes are complicated by a strong blend of absinthe and the barracks, Abraham and "the Zouzou" mingled, something fairy-tale-like and simply burlesque, like a page of the Old Testament related by Tommy Atkins.

A curious sight for those who have eyes that can see.

A wild and corrupted people whom we are civilising by teaching them our vices. The ferocious and uncontrolled authority of grotesque bashaws, who gravely use their *grand cordons* of the Legion of Honour as handkerchiefs, and for a mere yea or nay order a man to be bastinadoed. It is the justice of the conscienceless, bespectacled cadis under the palm-tree, Mawworms of the Koran and Law, who dream languidly of promotion and sell their decrees, as Esau did his birthright, for a dish of lentils or sweetened kouskous. Drunken and libertine cadis are they, formerly servants to some General Yusuf or the like, who get intoxicated on champagne, along with laundresses from Port Mahon, and fatten on roast mutton, whilst before their tents the whole tribe waste away with hunger, and fight with the harriers for the bones of the lordly feast.

All around spread the plains in waste, burnt grass, leafless shrubs, thickets of cactus and mastic—"the Granary of France!"—a granary void of grain, alas! and rich alone in vermin and jackals. Abandoned camps, frightened tribes fleeing from them and famine, they know not whither, and strewing the road with corpses. At long intervals French villages, with the dwellings in ruins, the fields untilled, the maddened locusts gnawing even the window-blinds, and all the settlers in the drinking-places, absorbing absinthe and discussing projects of reform and the Constitution.

This is what Tartarin might have seen had he given himself the trouble; but, wrapped up

entirely in his leonine-hunger, the son of Tarascon went straight on, looking to neither right
nor left, his eyes steadfastly fixed on the imaginary monsters which never really appeared.

As the shelter-tent was stubborn in not
unfolding, and the compressed meat-cakes
would not dissolve, the caravan was obliged
to stop, morn and eve, at tribal camps.
Everywhere, thanks to the gorgeous cap of
Prince Gregory, our hunters were welcomed
with open arms.   They lodged in the aghas'
odd palaces, large white windowless farm-
houses, where they found, pell-mell, narghilehs
and mahogany furniture, Smyrna carpets and
moderator lamps, cedar coffers full of Turkish
sequins, and French statuette-decked clocks
in the Louis Philippe style.

Everywhere, too, Tartarin was given splen-
drous galas, *diffas*, and *fantasias*, which, being
interpreted, mean feasts and circuses.   In his
honour whole *goums* blazed away powder,
and floated their burnouses in the sun.
When the powder was burnt, the agha would
come and hand in his bill.   This is what is
called Arab hospitality.

But always no lions, no more than on London Bridge.

Nevertheless, the Tarasconian did not grow disheartened. Ever bravely diving more deeply into the South, he spent the days in beating up the thickets, probing the dwarf-palms with the muzzle of his rifle, and saying " Boh ! " to every bush. And every evening, before lying down, he went into ambush for two or three hours. Useless trouble, however, for the lion did not show himself.

One evening, though, going on six o'clock, as the caravan scrambled through a violet-hued mastic-grove, where fat quails tumbled about in the grass, drowsy through the heat, Tartarin of Tarascon fancied he heard— though afar and very vague, and thinned down by the breeze—that wondrous roaring to which he had so often listened by Mitaine's Mena- gerie at home.

At first the hero feared he was dreaming ; but in an instant further the roaring recom- menced more distinct, although yet remote ; and this time the camel's hump shivered in terror, and made the tinned meats and arms in the cases rattle, whilst all the dogs in the camps were heard howling in every corner of the horizon.

Beyond doubt this was the lion.

Quick, quick! to the ambush. There was not a minute to lose.

Near at hand there happened to be an old *marabout's*, or saint's, tomb, with a white cupola, and the defunct's large yellow slippers placed in a niche over the door, and a mass of odd offerings—hems of blankets, gold thread, red hair—hung on the wall.

Tartarin of Tarascon left his prince and his camel and went in search of a good spot for lying in wait. Prince Gregory wanted to follow him, but the Tarasconian refused, bent on confronting Leo alone. But still he besought His Highness not to go too far away, and, as a measure of foresight, he entrusted him with his pocket-book, a good-sized one, full of precious papers and bank-notes, which he feared would get torn by the lion's claws. This done, our hero looked up a good place.

A hundred steps in front of the temple a

little clump of rose-laurel shook in the twilight haze on the edge of a rivulet all but dried up.

There it was that Tartarin went and ensconced himself, one knee on the ground, according to the regular rule, his rifle in his hand, and

his huge hunting-knife stuck boldly before
him in the sandy bank.

Night fell.

The rosy tint of nature changed into violet,
and then into dark blue. A petty pool of
clear water gleamed like a hand-glass over
the river-pebbles; this was the watering-place
of the wild animals.

On the other slope the whitish trail was
dimly to be discerned which their heavy
paws had traced in the brush—a mysterious
path which made one's flesh creep. Join to
this sensation that from the vague swarming sound in African forests, the swishing of
branches, the velvety pads of roving creatures,
the jackal's shrill yelp, and up in the sky, two
or three hundred feet aloft, vast flocks of
cranes passing on with screams like poor little
children having their weasands slit. You
will own that there were grounds for a man
being moved.

Tartarin was so, and even more than that,
for the poor fellow's teeth chattered, and on
the cross-bar of his hunting-knife, planted
upright in the bank, as we repeat, his rifle-

barrel rattled like a pair of castanets. Do
not ask too much of a man! There are times
when one is not in the mood ; and, moreover,
where would be the merit if heroes were
never afraid?

Well, yes, Tartarin was afraid, and all the
time, too, for the matter of that. Nevertheless, he held out for an hour ; better, for two ;
but heroism has its limits. Nigh him, in the
dry part of the rivulet-bed, the Tarasconian
unexpectedly heard the sound of steps and
of pebbles rolling. This time terror lifted
him off the ground. He banged away both
barrels at haphazard into the night, and re-
treated as fast as his legs would carry him to
the *marabout's* chapel-vault, leaving his knife
standing up in the sand like a cross com-
memorative of the grandest panic that ever
assailed the soul of a conqueror of hydras.

"Help! this way, *prance;* the lion is on
me!"

There was silence.

"*Prance, prance,* are you there?"

The prince was not there. On the white
moonlit wall of the fane the camel alone cast

the queer-shaped shadow of his protuberance.
Prince Gregory had cut and run with the
wallet of bank-notes.   His Highness had
been for the month past awaiting this oppor-
tunity.

VI.

Bagged him at Last.

IT was not until early on the morrow of this adventurous and dramatic eve that our hero awoke, and acquired assurance doubly sure that the prince and the treasure had really gone off, without any prospect of return. When he saw himself alone in the little white tomb-house, betrayed, robbed, abandoned in the heart of savage Algeria, with a one-humped camel and some pocket-money as all his resources, then did the

representative of Tarascon for the first time
doubt. He doubted Montenegro, friendship,
glory, and even lions; and the great man
blubbered bitterly.

Whilst he was pensively seated on the sill
of the sanctuary, holding his head between
his hands and his gun between his legs,
with the camel mooning at him, the thicket
over the way was divided, and the stupor-
stricken Tartarin saw a gigantic lion appear
not a dozen paces off. It thrust out its
high head and emitted powerful roars,
which made the temple walls shake beneath
their votive decorations, and even the saint's
slippers dance in their niche.

The Tarasconian alone did not tremble.

" At last you've come ! " he shouted, jumping up and levelling the rifle.

Bang, bang ! went a brace of shells into
its head.

It was done. For a minute, on the fiery
background of the Afric sky, there was a
dreadful firework display of scattered brains,
smoking blood, and tawny hair. When all
fell, Tartarin perceived two colossal negroes

furiously running towards him, brandishing
cudgels.   They were his two negro acquaintances of Milianah !

Oh, misery !
This was the domesticated lion, the poor
blind beggar of the Mohammed Monastery,

whom the Tarasconian's bullets had knocked over.

This time, spite of Mahound, Tartarin escaped neatly. Drunk with fanatical fury, the two African collectors would have surely beaten him to pulp had not the god of chase and war sent him a delivering angel in the shape of the rural constable of the Orléans-ville commune. By a bypath this *garde champêtre* came up, his sword tucked under his arm.

The sight of the municipal cap suddenly calmed the negroes' choler. Peaceful and majestic, the officer with the brass badge drew up a report on the affair, ordered the camel to be loaded with what remained of the king of beasts, and the plaintiffs as well as the delinquent to follow him, proceeding to Orléansville, where all was deposited with the law-courts receiver.

There issued a long and alarming case!

After the Algeria of the native tribes which he had overrun, Tartarin of Tarascon became thence acquainted with another Algeria, not less weird and to be dreaded—the Algeria in the towns, surcharged with lawyers and their papers. He got to know the pettifogger who does business at the back of a café—the legal Bohemian, with documents reeking of wormwood bitters and white neckcloths spotted with champoreau; the ushers, the attorneys, all the locusts of stamped paper, meagre and famished, who eat up the colonist body and boots—ay, to the very straps of them, and leave him peeled to the core like an Indian cornstalk, stripped leaf by leaf.

Before all else it was necessary to ascertain whether the lion had been killed on the civil or the military territory. In the former case the matter regarded the Tribunal of Commerce; in the second, Tartarin would be dealt with by the Council of War; and at the mere name the impressionable Tarasconian saw himself shot at the foot of the ramparts or huddled up in a casemate-silo.

The puzzle lay in the limitation of the two territories being very hazy in Algeria.

At length, after a month's running about, entanglements, and waiting under the sun in

the yards of Arab Departmental offices, it was
established that, whereas the lion had been
killed on the military territory, on the other
hand Tartarin was in the civil territory when
he shot. So the case was decided in the
civil courts, and our hero was let off on
paying two thousand five hundred francs
damages, costs not included.

How could he pay such a sum?

The few piastres escaped from the prince's
sweep had long since gone in legal documents and judicial libations. The unfortunate lion-destroyer was therefore reduced
to selling the store of guns by retail, rifle by
rifle; so went the daggers, the Malay kreeses,
and the life-preservers. A grocer purchased
the preserved aliments; an apothecary what
remained of the medicaments. The big
boots themselves walked off after the improved tent to a dealer of curiosities, who
elevated them to the dignity of "rarities
from Cochin-China."

When everything was paid up, only the
lion's skin and the camel remained to Tartarin. The hide he had carefully packed, to

be sent to Tarascon to the address of brave Commandant Bravida, and, later on, we shall see what came of this fabulous trophy. As for the camel, he reckoned on making

use of him to get back to Algiers, not by riding on him, but by selling him to pay his coach-fare—the best way to employ a camel in travelling. Unhappily the beast

P

was difficult to place, and no one would offer a copper for him.

Still Tartarin wanted to regain Algiers by hook or crook. He was in haste again to behold Baya's blue bodice, his little snuggery and his fountains, as well as to repose on the white trefoils of his little cloister whilst awaiting money from France. So our. hero did not hesitate; distressed but not downcast, he undertook to make the journey afoot and penniless by short stages.

In this enterprise the camel did not cast him off. The strange animal had taken an unaccountable fancy for his master, and on seeing him leave Orléansville, he set to striding steadfastly behind him, regulating his pace by his, and never quitting him by a yard.

At the first outset Tartarin found this touching; such fidelity and devotion above proof went to his heart, all the more because the creature was accommodating, and fed himself on nothing. Nevertheless, after a few days, the Tarasconian was worried by having this glum companion perpetually at

his heels, to remind him of his misadven-
tures. Ire arising, he hated him for his sad
aspect, hump and gait of a goose in harness.
To tell the whole truth, he held him as his
Old Man of the Sea, and only pondered on
how to shake him off; but the follower would
not be shaken off. Tartarin attempted to
lose him, but the camel always found him;
he tried to outrun him, but the camel ran
faster. He bade him begone, and hurled
stones at him. The camel stopped with a
mournful mien, but in a minute resumed the
pursuit, and always ended by overtaking him.
Tartarin had to resign himself.

For all that, when, after eight full days
of tramping, the dusty and harassed Tarasconian espied the first white housetops of
Algiers glimmer from afar in the verdure,
and when he got to the city gates on the
noisy Mustapha Avenue, amid the Zouaves,
Biskris, and Mahonnais, all swarming around
him and staring at him trudging by with his
camel, overtasked patience escaped him.

"No! no!" he growled, "it is not likely!
I cannot enter Algiers with such an animal!

Profiting by a jam of vehicles, he turned off into the fields and jumped into a ditch. In a minute or so he saw over his head on the highway the camel flying off with long strides and stretching his neck with a wistful air.

Relieved of a great weight thereby, the hero sneaked out of his covert, and entered the town anew by a circuitous path which skirted the wall of his own little garden.

VII.

Catastrophes upon Catastrophes.

ENTIRELY astonished was Tartarin before his Moorish dwelling when he stopped.

Day was dying and the street deserted. Through the low pointed-arch doorway which the negress had forgotten to close, laughter was heard; and the clink of wine-glasses, the popping of champagne corks; and, floating over all the jolly uproar, a feminine voice singing clearly and joyously:

> "Do you like, Marco la Bella,
> To dance in the hall hung with bloom?'

"Throne of heaven!" ejaculated the Tar-asconian, turning pale, as he rushed into the enclosure.

Hapless Tartarin! what a sight awaited him! Beneath the arches of the little cloister, amongst bottles, pastry, scattered cushions, pipes, tambourines, and guitars, Baya was singing "Marco la Bella" with a ship captain's cap over one ear. She had on no blue vest or bodice; indeed, her only wear was a silvery gauze wrapper and full pink trousers. At her feet, on a rug, surfeited with love and sweetmeats, Barbassou, the infamous skipper Barbassou, was bursting with laughter at hearing her.

The apparition of Tartarin, haggard, thinned, dusty, his flaming eyes, and the bristling up fez tassel, sharply interrupted this tender Turkish-Marseillais orgie. Baya piped the low whine of a frightened leveret, and ran for safety into the house. But Barbassou did not wince; he only laughed the louder, saying:

"Ha, ha, Monsieur Tartarin! What do you say to that now? You see she does know French."

Tartarin of Tarascon advanced furiously, crying:

"Captain!"

"*Digo-li qué vengué, moun bon!*—tell him what's happened, old dear!" screamed the Moorish woman, leaning over the first floor gallery with a pretty low-bred gesture.

The poor man, overwhelmed, let himself collapse upon a drum. His genuine Moorish beauty not only knew French, but the French of Marseilles!

"I told you not to trust the Algerian girls," observed Captain Barbassou sententiously. "They're as tricky as your Montenegrin prince."

Tartarin lifted his head.

"Do you know where the prince is?"

"Oh, he's not far off. He has gone to live five years in the handsome prison of Mustapha. The rogue let himself be caught with his hand in the pocket. Anyways, this is not the first time he has been clapped into the calaboose. His Highness has already done three years somewhere, and—stop a bit! I believe it was at Tarascon."

"At Tarascon!" cried out her worthiest

son, abruptly enlightened. "That's how he only knew one part of the town."

"Hey? Of course. Tarascon—a jail bird's-eye view from the state prison. I tell you, my poor Monsieur Tartarin, you have to keep your peepers jolly well skinned in this deuce of a country, or be exposed to very disagreeable things. For a sample, there's the muezzin's game with you."

"What game? Which muezzin?"

"Why your'n, of course! The chap across the way who is making up to Baya. That newspaper, the *Akbar*, told the yarn t'other day, and all Algiers is laughing over it even now. It is so funny for that steeplejack up aloft in his crow's-nest to make declarations of love under your very nose to the little beauty whilst singing out his prayers, and making appointments with her between bits of the Koran."

"Why, then, they're all scamps in this country!" howled the unlucky Tarasconian.

Barbassou snapped his fingers like a philosopher.

"My dear lad, you know, these new countries are 'rum!' But, anyhow, if you'll believe

me, you'd best cut back to Tarascon at full
speed."

"It's easy to say, 'Cut back.' Where's
the money to
come from?
Don't you know
that I was
plucked out
there in the
desert?"

"What does
that matter?"
said the captain
merrily. "The
Zouave sails to-
morrow, and if
you like I will
take you home.
Does that suit
you, mate? Ay?
Then all goes
well. You have
only one thing
to do. There are

some bottles of fizz left, and half the pie. Sit
you down and pitch in without any grudge."

After the minute's wavering which self-respect commanded, the Tarasconian chose his course manfully. Down he sat, and they touched glasses. Baya, gliding down at that chink, sang the finale of "Marco la Bella," and the jollification was prolonged deep into the night.

About 3 A.M., with a light head but a heavy foot, our good Tarasconian was returning from seeing his friend the captain off, when, in passing the mosque, the remembrance of his muezzin and his practical jokes made him laugh, and instantly a capital idea of revenge flitted through his brain.

The door was open. He entered, threaded long corridors hung with mats, mounted and kept on mounting till he finally found himself in a little oratory, where an openwork iron lantern swung from the ceiling, and embroidered an odd pattern in shadows upon the blanched walls.

There sat the crier on a divan, in his large turban and white pelisse, with his Mostaganam pipe, and a bumper of absinthe before him, which he whipped up in the orthodox manner, whilst awaiting the hour to call true believers to prayer. At view of Tartarin, he dropped his pipe in terror.

"Not a word, knave!" said the Tarasconian, full of his project. "Quick! Off with turban and coat!"

The Turkish priest-crier tremblingly handed over his outer garments, as he would have done with anything else. Tartarin donned them, and gravely stepped out upon the minaret platform.

In the distance the sea shone. The white roofs glittered in the moonbeams. On the sea breeze was heard the strumming of a few belated guitars. The Tarasconian muezzin gathered himself up for the effort during a space, and then, raising his arms, he set to chanting in a very shrill voice:

"*La Allah il Allah!* Mahomet is an old humbug! The Orient, the Koran, bashaws, lions, Moorish beauties—they are all not worth a fly's skip! There is nothing left but gammoners. Long live Tarascon!"

Whilst the illustrious Tartarin, in his queer jumbling of Arabic and Provençal, flung his mirthful maledictions to the four quarters, sea, town, plain and mountain, the clear,

solemn voices of the other muezzins answered
him, taking up the strain from minaret to
minaret, and the believers of the upper town
devoutly beat their bosoms.

VIII

Tarascon again !

MID-DAY has come.

The *Zouave* had her steam up, ready to go. Upon the balcony of the Valentin Café, high above, the officers were levelling telescopes, and, with the colonel at their head, looking at the lucky little craft that was going back to France. This is the main distraction of the staff. On the lower level, the roads glittered. The old Turkish cannon breaches, stuck up along the waterside, blazed in the sun. The passengers hurried. Biskris and Mahonnais piled their luggage up in the wherries.

Tartarin of Tarascon had no luggage. Here he comes down the Rue de la Marine through the little market, full of bananas and melons, accompanied by his friend Barbassou. The hapless Tarasconian left on the Moorish strand his gun-cases and his illusions, and now he had to sail for Tarascon with his hands in his otherwise empty pockets. He had barely leaped into the captain's cutter before a breathless beast slid down from the heights of the square and galloped towards him. It was the faithful camel, who had been hunting after his master in Algiers during the last four-and-twenty hours.

On seeing him, Tartarin changed counten-ance, and feigned not to know him, but the camel was not going to be put off. He scampered along the quay; he whinnied for his friend, and regarded him with affection.

"'Take me away," his sad eyes seemed to say, "take me away in your ship, far, far from

this sham Arabia, this ridiculous Land of the
East, full of locomotives and stage coaches,

where a camel is so sorely out of keeping
that I do not know what will become of
me. You are the last real Turk, and I am

the last camel.   Do not let us part, O my
Tartarin !"

" Is that camel yours ? " the captain inquired.

"Not a bit of it !" replied Tartarin, who
shuddered at the idea of entering Tarascon
with that ridiculous escort ; and, impudently
denying the companion of his misfortunes, he
spurned the Algerian soil with his foot, and
gave the cutter the shoving-off start.   The
camel sniffed of the water, extended its neck,
cracked its joints, and, jumping in behind the
row-boat at haphazard, he swam towards the
Zouave with his humpback floating like a
bladder, and his long neck projecting over
the wave like the beak of a galley.

Cutter and camel came alongside the mail
steamer together.

" This dromedary regularly cuts me up,"
observed Captain Barbassou, quite affected.
" I have a good mind to take him aboard
and make a present of him to the Zoological
Gardens at Marseilles."

And so they hauled up the camel with
many blocks and tackles upon the deck, being

increased in weight by the brine, and the
Zouave started.

Tartarin spent the two days of the crossing by himself in his stateroom, not because the sea was rough, or that the red fez

Q

had too much to suffer, but because the deuced camel, as soon as his master appeared above decks, showed him the most preposterous attentions. You never did see a camel make 'such an exhibition of a man as this.

From hour to hour, through the cabin portholes, where he stuck out his nose now and then, Tartarin saw the Algerian blue sky pale away; until one morning, in a silvery fog, he heard with delight Marseilles bells ringing out. The *Zouave* had arrived and cast anchor.

Our man, having no luggage, got off without saying anything, hastily slipped through Marseilles for fear he was still pursued by the camel, and never breathed till he was in a third-class carriage making for Tarascon.

Deceptive security!

Hardly were they two leagues from the city before every head was stuck out of window. There were outcries and astonishment. Tartarin looked in his turn, and— what did he descry! the camel, reader, the inevitable camel, racing along the line behind the train, and keeping up with it!

The dismayed Tartarin drew back and shut his eyes.

After this disastrous expedition of his he had reckoned on slipping into his house *incognito.* But the presence of this burden-some quadruped rendered the thing impossible. What kind of a triumphal entry would he make? Good heavens! not a sou, not a lion, nothing to show for it save a camel!

"Tarascon! Tarascon!"

He was obliged to get down.

O amazement!

Scarce had the hero's red fez popped out of the doorway before a loud shout of "Tartarin for ever!" made the glazed roof of the railway station tremble. "Long life to Tartarin, the lion-slayer!" And out burst the windings of horns and the choruses of the local musical societies.

Tartarin felt death had come: he believed in a hoax. But, no! all Tarascon was there, waving their hats, all of the same way of thinking. Behold the brave Commandant Bravida, Costecalde the armourer, the Chief Judge, the chemist, and the whole noble corps of cap-poppers, who pressed around their leader, and carried him in triumph out through the passages.

Singular effects of the mirage !—the hide of the blind lion sent to Bravida was the cause of all this riot. With that humble fur exhibited in the club-room, the Tarasconians, and, at the back of them, the whole South of France, had grown exalted. The *Sémaphore* newspaper had spoken of it. A drama had been invented. It was not merely a solitary lion which Tartarin had slain, but ten, nay, twenty—pooh ! a herd of lions had been made marmalade of. Hence, on disembarking at Marseilles, Tartarin was already celebrated without being aware of it, and an enthusiastic telegram had gone on before him by two hours to his native place.

But what capped the climax of the popular gladness was to see a fancifully shaped animal, covered with foam and dust, appear behind the hero, and stumble down the station stairs.

Tarascon for an instant believed that its dragon was come again.

Tartarin set his fellow-citizens at ease.

"'This is my camel," he said.

Already feeling the influence of the splendid sun of Tarascon, which makes people tell "bouncers" unwittingly, he added, as he fondled the camel's hump :

"It is a noble beast! It saw me kill all my lions!"

Whereupon he familiarly took the arm of the commandant, who was red with pleasure ; and followed by his camel, surrounded by the cap-hunters, acclaimed by all the population, he placidly proceeded towards the Baobab Villa ; and, on the march, thus commenced the account of his mighty hunting :

"Once upon an evening, you are to imagine that, out in the depths of the Sahara "——-

A
TARTARIN
SES CONCITOYENS

www.ingramcontent.com/pod-product-compliance
Lightning Source LLC
Chambersburg PA
CBHW021959050726
47498CB00006BA/1923